M000080472

## His kiss was hard, demanding her response

Jenna plunged both hands against Sam's chest, desperate to wrench herself free.

"Get out," she ordered in a vicious tone. "And don't *ever* try that again."

Sam arched his brows. "Aren't you overreacting? It was only a kiss thanks to the speed with which you flung me aside."

"And what if I hadn't?" she retorted, hastily adding, "I happen to believe in the sanctity of marriage."

"Good, that makes two of us."

Sam swung from the room, and Jenna sank down on the bed, her mind whirling. Her husband had required little in the way of physical affection, and over the years Jenna had learned to control her responses.

Sam would demand more than Jenna was prepared, or able, to give.

## Books by Elizabeth Oldfield

HARLEQUIN PRESENTS

These books may be available at your local bookseller.

For a free catalog listing all titles currently available,
send your name and address to:

Harlequin Reader Service
P.O. Box 52040, Phoenix, AZ 85072-2040
Canadian address: Stratford, Ontario N5A 6W2

# ELIZABETH OLDFIELD

## fighting lady

*Harlequin Books*

TORONTO • NEW YORK • LONDON
AMSTERDAM • PARIS • SYDNEY • HAMBURG
STOCKHOLM • ATHENS • TOKYO • MILAN

Harlequin Presents first edition April 1984
ISBN 0-373-10685-8

Original hardcover edition published in 1984
by Mills & Boon Limited

Copyright © 1984 by Elizabeth Oldfield. All rights reserved.
Philippine copyright 1984. Australian copyright 1984.
Except for use in any review, the reproduction or utilization of
this work in whole or in part in any form by any electronic,
mechanical or other means, now known or hereafter invented,
including xerography, photocopying and recording, or in any
information storage or retrieval system, is forbidden without
the permission of the publisher, Harlequin Enterprises Limited,
225 Duncan Mill Road, Don Mills, Ontario, Canada M3B 3K9.

All the characters in this book have no existence outside the
imagination of the author and have no relation whatsoever to
anyone bearing the same name or names. They are not even
distantly inspired by any individual known or unknown to the
author, and all the incidents are pure invention.

The Harlequin trademarks, consisting of the words
HARLEQUIN PRESENTS and the portrayal of a Harlequin,
are trademarks of Harlequin Enterprises Limited and are
registered in the Canada Trade Marks Office; the portrayal
of a Harlequin is registered in the United States Patent
and Trademark Office.

Printed in U.S.A.

# CHAPTER ONE

ANOTHER red light.

'Hell and damnation!' Jenna muttered, slamming her foot on the brake pedal to force the Mini to a reluctant halt. Ahead the city street unravelled to the horizon, each intersection jealously guarded by a phalanx of traffic lights. She totted up the number that lay between her and the multi-storey car park—six sets at least, and what was the betting each would capriciously leap to red on her approach! In mute frustration she pounded the steering wheel with the flat of her hand. The meeting was scheduled for ten o'clock and already her watch showed nine forty-five. Hissed entreaties at the cars crossing her vision produced no miracles; indeed they positively dawdled, as if to emphasise that her fate this morning was to get nowhere—fast!

How Herbert would savour her late arrival, particularly with a captive audience listening in. He would brandish it as further proof that women were incompatible with the cut-and-thrust of daily journalism. Herbert Holt, editor of *The View*, an upmarket London newspaper, was an obnoxious, self-important Napoleon, Jenna decided with feeling. Unfortunately he was also a shrewd businessman with a lifetime's experience of the newspaper world and that, coupled to a virulent male chauvinism, made him a force to be reckoned with. In his opinion only a fool let women loose in newspaper offices, except in the capacity of tea-girl or tucked away on the 'Women's Page' where the harm they did could be kept to a minimum. That Jenna dared to be a political reporter, and a good one, meant she was a constant aggravation and fair game for his vitriolic tongue.

Finally the cross traffic petered out, the lights turned to amber, but as she reached for the gear lever Jenna was distracted by an ear-splitting squeal and her small car was rammed from behind. The impact flung her against the steering wheel. There was a frantic judder as the Mini fought its brakes, a crunch, a splatter of falling glass, and then uncanny silence. Winded, she gulped several times, blue eyes wide with shock, and after a moment pushed herself upright, running an unsteady hand through her sheaf of ash-blonde curls.

'Are you all right?' A young man, his features nipped pale by the cold, was peering anxiously through the windscreen.

Taking a deep breath, Jenna struggled out into the January chill. An icy blast, peppered with flecks of sleet, caught her unawares and she hastily tugged the collar of her fleecy-lined jacket closer around her neck. 'What do you think you're playing at?' she demanded, stalking round to survey the damage.

Her knees might be shaking, but she was unhurt, only furious that some mindless fool had careered into her car causing unnecessary trouble, expense and now making her even later for Herbert's damned meeting. One of the rearlights was smashed to smithereens and the back bumper had a slight dent. When she realised that the taxi which had hit her showed no sign of damage at all, her lips compressed into a tight line. 'It isn't fair!' she wanted to yell. But how much in life was fair?

'You're sure you're okay?' the taxi-driver asked again, though he was cheerful now.

Her flashing eyes and tempestuous stance—hands on hips, foot tapping irritably—were proof she was unharmed. Unharmed and quite a looker! She was a tall girl, slender in trousers and a battered leather flying-jacket, tousled blonde curls blowing about her shoulders as she bent to inspect the damage. And as she bent her soft cream leather trousers stretched over her rear end in a way that made his palm itch.

'It shouldn't cost much to mend, ducks,' he smiled, squatting close beside her. 'In any case, my insurance will pay.'

Jenna was in no mood to be easily appeased. 'And how am I supposed to manage while my car's being repaired?' she retorted. 'I go out to work and I have a small child, my transport is essential.'

A small child—so married, the taxi-driver deduced. Oh well, you can't win 'em all. 'The car will only be off the road for a day or two,' he coaxed, standing upright to fumble inside his anorak. 'Here's my card. Send me the bill when the damage has been fixed and I'll post back a cheque by return of post. Sorry about the bump, I must have been day-dreaming.'

'Huh!' Jenna snorted, with as much severity as she could muster. Her anger was faltering for, in truth, the damage was trivial; an irritation rather than a calamity.

Five minutes later she was on the move once more, keeping a wary eye on her rear-view mirror. Now she was destined to be well and truly behind schedule for Herbert's get-together in the boardroom. He had termed it a 'forward planning meeting', but what did he have up his sleeve this time? she wondered, waiting in line to enter the car park. Something unpleasant, no doubt. Something which would play havoc with her rigorously protected routine, for when he had mentioned the meeting, marching into her cubicle to choke it with the pungent aroma of aftershave, there had been a malicious gleam in his eye. Probably he would demand she travel, for he was well aware of her reluctance to leave the city. Jenna's winged brows pulled together. The party political conferences were safely out of the way until next autumn, what else was there? Only a by-election, but that was close at hand.

She had coped with the three conferences and

necessary time away from home by off-loading
Christopher on to Mrs Millet, her stalwart babyminder
in London, and by later depositing him with her parents
in Manchester. Her fingers tightened on the wheel. The
whole episode revived disturbing memories, for her son
had sobbed when she had left him, tearing her heart to
shreds. Months later Mrs Millet confessed she had
found the responsibility of looking after an energetic
two-year-old to be quite a strain and, as expected, the
arrangement had provoked her mother into repeating
the old arguments against Jenna's career *ad nauseam*.

'Edward would never have approved,' her mother had
sniffed, shadowing Christopher with a dustpan to catch
the biscuit crumbs before they hit her pristine carpet. 'If
you were sensible and moved back to Manchester you
could live nicely on the money he left. You wouldn't be
rich, I admit, but you could manage. Why you persist in
this fight for independence, I'll never know.'

Jenna had held her tongue. Time and again she had
tried to explain her feelings, but it was beyond her
mother's comprehension that anyone should wish to
raise an infant son on a single-parent basis *and* have a
career, in preference to existing quietly as a housewife.

Reaching the barrier, she stretched out an arm, biting
the ticket between her teeth as the bar lifted and she
swung onto the concrete ramp. The ground floor space
was full, and the second, and the third. Minutes rushed
by as she motored up and up, taking the corners like an
Alpine rally driver in her search for a vacant space.
Success at last, and then there were several flights of
stone stairs to hurtle down before she reached street
level again. Face flushed, Jenna huddled deeper into
her jacket and dived breathlessly into the crush of
shoppers. The sleet was heavier now and, too late, she
remembered that her umbrella was still in the car. If
only she had been able to park at the newspaper offices,
but in order to grab one of the bays in the cramped

yard you had to reach them before nine o'clock, and rarely did she manage that.

But today she was much later than usual. Today the gods had decided it was time to slap her down, a direct result, Jenna thought ruefully, of her smug satisfaction the previous evening. Then she had been reviewing all she had achieved since Edward's death and had given herself a private pat on the back, a series of pats, if she was honest. Suddenly the frenetic days, the lonely nights, the strains and stresses of functioning alone in a world geared to married couples, were paying dividends. She had yet to reach the peak of success, but, for the time being, she was on a satisfying plateau. Christopher was happy and healthy, her name as a journalist had gained a measure of solid respect in political circles and, after months of practice, her photography showed promise. The most recent batch of snaps she had taken, albeit of her son, were excellent. Jenna felt the time was now approaching when she would be in a position to tell Herbert Holt exactly what she thought of him—as if he did not already know!—and sweep out of his employ to begin afresh as a freelance photo-journalist. With photography as her second string she would be able to support Christopher and herself with a modicum of style *and* run her life to suit them both. No longer would she have an employer breathing down her neck, no longer would she be liable to be ordered away, leaving her son desolate. But not yet. Freelancing was a major step, one which needed to be approached with caution. Jenna had to know that her photographs would sell, and sell well, before casting aside the security of *The View* and her regular pay cheque.

Head down, she hitched her soft suede duffle-bag further on to her shoulder, grimacing against the sleet. Yesterday evening she had been smug, but today's events were a reminder that life was still a battlefield. Her problems had begun small. Firstly the milkman had neglected to deliver the usual pinta, so Christopher had had to eat dry cornflakes and go without his mug of warm chocolate; not that he had worried, yet Jenna felt guilty. Big guilts she coped with on a regular basis, but little guilts were an added burden. As a working mother she wanted to do her very best for her son, and so the missed milk rankled.

Next she had been calling Christopher from the foot of the stairs, urging him to hurry because she was poised to leave, when he had knocked against a pot plant on the low landing windowsill. En route to her feet the pot had bounced on every single step, scattering soil from top to bottom of the staircase. Clenching her fists, she had fought the desire to leap up and down in mindless rage and instead had lunged for the vacuum cleaner and wasted precious time clearing up the mess. Finally, on reaching playschool, Christopher had reverted to his younger days by throwing himself against her, clinging on for dear life and demanding that she must not leave him.

'But Mrs Millet will collect you at twelve, darling,' she had explained, attempting to prise his little arms from around her neck. 'And Mummy will be home just after five.'

Limpet-like he had stuck to her, his tears staining the shoulder of her jacket, until one of the teachers had pulled him from her, shrieking and wriggling, and she had made a dive for the door. Once outside she had stopped, listening to his wails until a tight lump formed in her chest and she had felt like wailing, too. Jenna had driven away, persuading herself that his tears would vanish as abruptly as they had started, but when she discovered his teddy-bear still tucked into her duffle-bag, her heart had quaked afresh. Christopher adored his teddy and despite having covered several miles, she was tempted to U-turn. But Herbert Holt swept down on her misdemeanours like a vulture and she could not risk being noticeably late too often. Now, ironically, it seemed that had she turned back to the playschool she might have avoided the collision . . .

Marching into the vestibule of *The View*'s offices, Jenna stuck an impatient finger on the lift call button, using the hiatus to tuck her errant mustard-and-white checked shirt more firmly into her trousers. As the lift rose she searched in her duffle-bag for her comb, but drew a blank, and had to resort to running both hands through her hair and shaking the wind-tossed curls back into place. One of these days she would tip out her bag and ruthlessly dispose of three-quarters of the mind-boggling array she humped around. There were tissues and baby lotion, lipgloss which she regularly forgot to use, some notebooks and pencils, a tape recorder, building cubes, a bottle of cologne, Christopher's spare cardigan—and now a teddy-bear! Tucking a protruding furry arm out of sight, she tightened the drawstring. If anyone discovered she was toting around a one-eyed teddy-bear awkward questions might arise, and Herbert would love to play at inquisitor.

The boardroom was on the sixth floor, a utilitarian room furnished with an oval mahogany table, chairs upholstered in maroon and cream brocade, and a long sideboard which had three telephones at one end and a collection of bottles at the other. Stark winter light flooded in through large windows and when Jenna popped her head around the door she saw that everyone else was already installed. Her heart sank.

'Well, well, if Jenna Devine hasn't decided to honour us with her presence!' Herbert rumbled as she entered. 'Dressed by courtesy of Oxfam as usual, or is the Salvation Army in vogue this year?'

'I'm not the twinset and pearls type,' she ground out from between her teeth. Only since Edward's death had she dressed to suit herself, and she was damned if she would take a retrograde step on Herbert Holt's account!

'Do sit down,' he said facetiously, with a sweep of his pudgy hand. 'I'm so delighted that you managed to fit us in. Doing something vital, were you, like polishing your cutlery?'

'I apologise for being late, but I had a bump in the car,' she returned, keeping her voice deadly even. Everybody was listening and she loathed to be the centre of attention, especially playing Judy to Herbert's Punch.

'Women drivers!' he remarked patronisingly, showing a mock grimace to his audience and drawing a chorus of chuckles.

'I was slammed in the backside by a *man*!' she flared, her high-heeled boots rapping across the parquet floor as she made for the one vacant chair.

'Wish it had been me,' the Sports Editor inserted, raising more amusement.

Promptly Herbert became businesslike; he preferred to make the jokes himself. Leaning back, he placed his fingertips magisterially together and waited until all heads were turned his way before deigning to speak. He was a short, silver-haired man in his late fifties, rather a fussy dresser, as his Paisley-patterned cravat, striped shirt and Prince-of-Wales checked threepiece suit indicated.

'As you all are aware, it is now some two years since Mr Kirby Desborough-Finch bought controlling shares in *The View*, and during that time circulation has broken all records, thanks to a steady hand at the helm.'

Herbert meant himself, everyone knew that. Off the cuff he invariably referred to Mr Kirby Desborough-Finch as 'that damned Aussie', but Jenna noted that this morning the owner was being allowed his full name and the correct degree of respect. Respect was warranted, for Mr Desborough-Finch owned a portfolio of newspapers, radio and television stations encircling the globe, and whenever he flew in to discuss his British interests Herbert was to be found at his elbow, murmuring 'Yes, sir' and 'No, sir' all day long.

Jenna slid on to her chair. The meeting must have barely started, for writing pads and sharpened pencils lay untouched before each one of the ten participants. Following form, Herbert now indulged in a barely disguised monologue of self-congratulation, so she guessed she had missed nothing of importance. Under cover of his words, she pushed her bag beneath her chair and began shrugging from the heavy leather jacket. When a tanned hand reached out to assist, she turned to smile her thanks. Jenna's wideset-blue eyes met dark brown ones, and clung there. Her heart skipped a beat. An unexpected *frisson* snatched at her senses and the man appeared to recognise that he had caught her off balance, for he smiled broadly, his teeth strong and white. Abstractedly it registered that he had a tiny gap between the front upper two. Seated among the pale English winter faces he resembled a vibrant sun-god, making everyone else fade to insignificance. Who was he? His sculpted face was tanned to a sultry gold, while his hair was a blend of dark and light, bleached almost platinum at the tips. It was unstylishly long, flopping across his wide brow. He was obviously a man who suited himself and, like her, was casually dressed, wearing a brown sheepskin jacket over a sweater and pair of shabby peat-brown corduroy trousers. An arrogant beaky nose prevented him from being handsome, but he did not look like a man who set much store on his appearance; there was more in life to interest him than his own reflection. Jenna wondered what lay behind his calm exterior and tranquil dark eyes, for he was lazily answering her smile, paying not one speck of attention to Herbert who continued to drone on at the far end of the table.

With an effort she dragged her eyes from him and

stared down at her hands. What on earth was happening? She had spent minutes grinning at a complete stranger like a besotted schoolgirl! Surprise rippled through her, for something behind his smile had revived a feeling she had long believed to be dead. But the years with Edward had taught her how to protect herself, and Jenna dismissed the emotion for the froth it was. Now, three years after her husband's death, she was in control of her life once more and the blueprint she had drawn up to cover the next few years took no account of men in any way, shape or form, be it sun-god or whatever. Ash-blonde hair blinkered her expression as Jenna fought against memories which irrationally surfaced; memories of how she had once yearned for Edward's love and how he had doled it out in frugal portions until, one way or another, she had reached her present state.

A hefty sand-coloured suede boot nudged her ankle and Jenna snapped up her head to glare at the stranger. How dared he shoot darts into her defences with such surprising ease and now take the liberty of playing footsie! A glimmer of amusement shone in the dark brown eyes which surveyed her, and she found his nonchalance disturbing. But his nudge had had a purpose, for she abruptly realised Herbert was tapping his pencil on the table, waiting for an answer.

'Lost your tongue, Jenna?' he smirked.

She swallowed hard. She had been too engrossed in the stranger and her subsequent thoughts to follow the path of his recital.

'Speaking as an outsider, I must confess I find your idea intriguing. It has possibilities,' the man beside her intervened in an Australian accent. He was rescuing her, and Jenna shot him a weak smile. 'Switching roles on an experimental basis will put everyone on their toes, that's for sure, though whether there's anything to be gained in the long run by asking political journalists to report on show business and vice versa, I have my doubts.'

'I don't fancy covering rugby,' one of the fashion writers complained.

'But I do fancy writing articles on sexy underwear,' the Sports Editor leered. 'Just watch me handpick those models!'

Everyone laughed. Now Jenna was alert. It appeared Herbert had come up with the idea of several of the journalists cross-functioning on a one-off basis, and that she had been detailed to cover the show business scene.

'What's news fodder in politics right now?' asked Shelagh, the gossip columnist who had been handed Jenna's department.

'There's a by-election pending in Kent which promises to be a real cliff-hanger.'

Shelagh fiddled with a stud ear-ring. 'How can you find *that* interesting?' she asked, noting Jenna's enthusiasm.

'But it is,' Jenna returned, experiencing a pang of regret that she would not be witnessing the excitement of voting day.

'Sort out details later,' Herbert interrupted, clearing his throat loudly to remind everyone that *he* wielded the power. Several side discussions obediently faded. 'We'll keep to broad outlines for now.' He went round the table listing the various changes and when he reached Jenna, he paused dramatically. She waited for the worst, and it came. 'Paris,' he announced. 'I'm assigning you to cover Vivienne Valdis and the premiere of her latest film. The woman has hit the headlines after years in the wilderness—apparently she's been reborn, and it's your job to discover how and why. You will follow her activities over a three-week period and submit copy for a two-part in-depth profile to be featured in the Sunday colour supplement.'

Jenna was suspended between pleasure and pain. Colour supplement exposure was a bite at the cherry she would be foolish to reject, but Paris! Once more she was being forced to abandon Christopher.

'How long in Paris?' she asked warily.

The editor wafted a vague hand. 'A few days.'

'And where does Vivienne Valdis live?' she demanded of Shelagh, praying it would not turn out to be Hollywood.

'Here, in Chelsea.'

A few days in Paris and then back home. Jenna's mind buzzed. Was it feasible for her to make the trip? Would Mrs Millet oblige? How might Christopher be affected?

'Chin up,' someone said softly, and when Jenna glanced sideways the suntanned stranger winked encouragement.

Plainly her shield had slipped to reveal her indecision, and she straightened her shoulders. 'That'll be fine,' she said with a firmness which was supposed to convince herself as much as Herbert.

'Your mother isn't likely to be stricken down?' he suggested.

She shook her head. Once, on her arrival at *The View* nine months ago, Christopher had been off colour and she had wheedled her way out of a couple of assignments abroad by concocting an elaborate tale about her mother's supposed illness; a tale Herbert had viewed with acute suspicion, but had been forced to accept.

'The old lady is in good health?' he persisted, his lip lifting in sarcasm.

'She's fine.'

Jenna had portrayed her mother as frail and ancient, tottering from one crisis to the next, clinging to life by a mere thread, whereas, in reality, her mother was a brisk fifty-five, bustling from Inner Wheel meetings to flower arranging to coffee mornings without pause, a circuit she regarded as tailor-made for her only daughter.

'She won't have a relapse?' Herbert sounded disappointed.

'Nothing is one hundred per cent certain,' Jenna said, seeing it would be wise to leave an escape hatch in case Christopher caught measles, or fractured a collarbone, or . . .

'Smile,' the man beside her entreated.

Herbert consulted his clipboard, obviously realising he had made all available headway. 'And you'll go along to take the photographs, Sam.' It was a statement, not a question, and Jenna could tell the matter had been prearranged.

'With pleasure,' the sun-god named Sam grinned.

He had pushed back his chair to flex legs which took up most of the available space beneath their end of the table and Jenna tucked her feet under her chair, determined not to allow him another nudge.

'You know Vivienne Valdis from the past?'

Herbert was asking for confirmation which he received from a quick dip of the sunbleached head.

'Just good friends?' the Sports Editor chortled.

He was winning more than his fair share of the laughs this morning, for another smatter of amusement greeted his trite observation. Vivienne Valdis' reputation was notorious, though how much was gossip column blah and how much was the truth, it was difficult to tell. The actress was a redhead with voluptuous curves, baby-soft voice and a lived-in past. A number of blue movies had launched her career, but a lean spell had occurred when she disappeared in total from the public eye. Now she was once again making films, but respectable films this time, and was trotting out the hackneyed plea of wishing to be known for her acting skills and not her naked body.

'Viv and I are like brother and sister,' the sun-god grinned amiably.

'With a spot of incest on the side?' the Sports Editor prompted.

There was a shrug in reply, nothing more. Jenna noticed that the sun-god was doodling. He had written something in capital letters on his pad and was busily adding surrealistic squiggles and shapes.

'I don't think you've met Sam, have you, Jenna?' Herbert intervened, squashing the general amusement with a scowl. 'Jenna Devine, meet Sam Wood from Down Under.' The two-tone head dipped again and the dark eyes smiled a greeting. 'Sam'll be taking all the photographs—and I mean *all*, so don't get any ideas beyond your station.'

Jenna felt a rush of pique. Her pictures were good. Grudgingly Herbert had allowed them to accompany one or two of her articles when, for some reason, a photographer had been unavailable. They had been black and white portraits, taking up a couple of column inches at most, nevertheless the definition had been clear and they were well angled. Jenna had been proud of them.

'Sam's a professional,' the editor said heavily. She glared along the table. Herbert was making an unfair comparison, because wasn't she almost a professional herself? 'So he's the boss. Any policy decisions and Sam makes them—understand?'

'Yes,' she snapped, glaring at Sam now, but he was untroubled, still engrossed in his doodling.

Why should he be designated the boss? she fumed inwardly. He's nothing but a half-cocked photographer, some beer-drinking buddy of Kirby Desborough-Finch's. Doubtless he had wangled a free trip over to Europe to meet up with Vivienne Valdis, who sounded to be an ex-girl-friend. The lean Australian relaxed further into his chair, and as the light altered she realised there was at least a day's growth of stubble on his jaw, dark stubble which contrasted with the sunbleached hair. My God! she thought, Herbert may not approve of my random appearance, but this character is ten times worse. Just what role does he play?

'Do you work for a newspaper in Australia?' she hissed when the editor's interest was deflected.

'No. For the past six months I've been living on an island on the Great Barrier Reef.'

The reply was no surprise, for his tan was burned deep and he exhibited the totally relaxed attitude of someone who has no deadlines to meet, no responsibilities. Such an easygoing air dismayed her. Where would he find the discipline to work to her orderly routine? Her sole intent was to keep the visit abroad to a minimum. He could waste as much time as he liked when they returned to London, but the Paris trip must be strictly in and out. She had no intention of swanning around with some beach bum from Australia.

'Any further questions?' demanded Herbert. There was silence. 'Right, we'll finish now. All those exchanging roles, please do your homework. I don't want any sloppy reporting, no mistakes, glaring or otherwise. What I'm looking for is fresh angles, a different approach. Understand?' A murmur of assent travelled around the table. 'There are two weeks before the change-over, so in the meantime pool your resources and we'll have another meeting next Friday to chew over any problems.' He adjusted his cravat with calm deliberation. 'And, my lovely Mrs Devine,' he said, giving her the benefit of a syrupy smile, 'it would be heartwarming if you'd make a special effort to be here on time.'

Having had the last word, he swept from the room.

'That man!' Jenna muttered savagely.

'You're *Mrs* Devine?' Sam questioned, tearing a sheet of paper from his pad and crushing it into a ball with one squeeze of his large fist.

She nodded, realising that, owing to the trauma that morning, she had neglected to wear her wedding ring. 'One of these days I'll tell that pompous little garden gnome exactly what to do with himself!' she threatened, boiling with resentment at Herbert's final thrust.

He had made it sound as though she was perpetually unreliable, which was not true. Heavens, if he only realised the efforts she made to keep appointments, rushing Christopher here, there and everywhere! Christopher, she thought, her eyes growing soft at the image of her own private little miracle, but if Herbert ever discovered she had a child he would then be able to oust her from *The View*. Jenna had known from the start that company policy banned working mothers, but the opportunity to work for such a high-class newspaper had been too good to miss, so she had kept silent about her son's existence.

Chairs scraped, people began to drift away. Someone came to chat with the Australian and Shelagh appeared at Jenna's elbow.

'I need help,' she moaned. 'I don't have the first idea about politics.'

'Don't worry, you'll manage fine,' Jenna smiled, and proceeded to give a thumbnail sketch of the forthcoming by-election. When she had allayed Shelagh's most immediate fears she asked about Vivienne Valdis.

'She's elusive,' the gossip-columnist said. 'Her career was launched by a manager, Gavrick Seymour. He was a Svengali type who never allowed her to say two honest words in succession. Now she's shaken free of him, but a creepy publicity agent hangs round to vet every single sentence. I suspect that beneath the glamour image Vivienne has the same feelings as you and I, but no one is ever given the chance to find out.' She jerked her head at Sam, now in the throes of ending his conversation. 'If *he* knows her from way back perhaps he'll be able to ease your way.' With that the girl departed.

Ripping off a sheet from her pad, Jenna frowned at the vague notes and decided that several hours' research were vital.

'Why didn't you give Holt the two-fingered salute and tell him where to get off?' the Australian asked, flicking aside his crumpled ball of paper.

'If only it was that easy!'

'I don't understand why he hired you in the first place when you so obviously make him prickle,' he said, unbuttoning his jacket and heaving it aside in order to slide one tanned hand into the trouser pocket at his hip. Jenna watched the action unwittingly, for he moved with an ease which was attractive. The Aran sweater beneath his thick sheepskin coat was as well worn as his trousers.

'Sorry to look such a scruff,' he grinned, following her gaze and making her eyes bounce guiltily away.

Jenna's cheeks grew hot. It was ages since she had even *noticed* a man as a male animal, but all of a sudden she was searingly aware of the manner in which the tight cords moulded his thighs, the thirteen stone of solid muscle lounging beside her. She bent her head, pretending to peer inside her bag.

'I didn't anticipate this visit to England,' he explained. 'One minute I was sweating cheerfully beneath the blazing sun and the next I found myself pitchforked into the middle of your winter. Keeping warm was my priority, so I unearthed this lot.' His dark eyes swept down his long body. 'It's been a while since I've worn them and I confess I hadn't realised how disreputable they are. I guess I'll have to re-equip.'

'Yes,' she agreed weakly.

'Why did Holt hire you?' he repeated, showing no wish to follow the last stragglers who were making for the door.

'He didn't, hence his antagonism. Mr Desborough-Finch was responsible.'

'How come?' He sounded genuinely interested.

'I'd done some freelance work for *The View* under a pseudonym and Herbert wrote to me, overflowing with praise, and suggesting we meet to discuss a fulltime contract.' Jenna chuckled at the memory and picked up her pencil, revolving it between tapered fingers. 'When I arrived and he realised I was female, he nearly had a heart attack!'

'You were dressed like that?' Sam's grin was sliding into a broad smile.

'Well, the weather wasn't stormy and I wasn't so bedraggled, but basically, yes.' Jenna shrugged. 'I was wearing trousers, I usually do, they're practical when you have a small . . .' She stopped dead.

'A small backside and legs up to your armpits,' he suggested, brown eyes sparkling.

'I was going to say a small car.' She wasn't. She had been going to say a small boy, but had realised her mistake just in time. Not a single soul at the newspaper was aware of Christopher's existence, it was safer that way. 'I wore a grey flannel trouser suit and a silk blouse with a big floppy bow. It was a fashionable outfit, but Herbert doesn't consider women are suited to political journalism, no matter how they're dressed. He prefers them to stay in the kitchen.'

'Or in the bedroom, flat on their backs.'

The outspoken comment and all its ramifications caught her napping. 'Yes, I suppose so,' she gulped. 'Because I was unexpectedly female Herbert was forced to switch horses midstream and he began promoting some flabby post in the fashion department when Mr Desborough-Finch arrived out of the blue. He's a very friendly type——'

'I know.'

'And he began chatting, asking about my work, eager to know what I was doing there.' A thought crossed Jenna's mind. 'Are you a friend of his?'

Sam rubbed at a sideburn. 'Not exactly . . . well, yes.' He paused, sorting out his answer. 'Let's just say I know him.'

Jenna continued with her tale. 'The upshot was that he didn't give a damn that I was a woman——'

'He'd like it, especially the legs up to the armpits.'

She grinned, curiously pleased at the compliment. 'And so I was hired to cover politics, much to Herbert's dismay. He prevaricated like mad, but Mr Desborough-Finch made it clear that if my reporting was good, I was a permanent addition. Fortunately my work is acceptable, even to Herbert, nevertheless he'd prefer to have a man in my job. If he could unseat me, he would. But Mr Desborough-Finch has been an invaluable support. He always comes to see me in my office——'

'—and your legs.'

'—whenever he visits. I know that should Herbert become too cranky I can always appeal for help, and Herbert knows that, too. So we shadow-box, though he does manage to hit a few sly punches home,' she admitted. 'But Mr Desborough-Finch's backing is a comfort.'

'He's a good sort,' Sam agreed, then leant back folding his arms. 'Why don't you want to go to Paris?'

'I do,' she declared stiffly, disliking his perspicacity.

He tilted his head to one side. 'Is it me you object to?'

The question was asked without rancour. He wasn't the type to be mortally offended if she had said yes, but his presence was secondary.

'I don't object to you.' Jenna abandoned the pencil and lifted her duffle-bag to her knees, fidgeting with the ties.

'Family problems?'

'Yes.' She thrust the word in hurriedly.

'I see.'

He did not see at all, but at least he had the sense not

to ask further, which was as well, for Jenna was not prepared to reveal her anxieties to a stranger, although his friendly manner seemed to invite confidences. She pulled herself up short. Ever since Edward had died she had kept well away from any man who was remotely attractive, and yet, within minutes, this layabout from the other side of the world had managed to grab her attention. He was a drifter, a no-good, she convinced herself, covertly eyeing the shadowed jaw. What worthwhile man of his age, which she guessed to be early thirties, would idle his life away lazing on a tropical island? She was not impressed. Probably he was no great shakes as a photographer either. Maybe she should take some snaps of Vivienne Valdis herself, in case his turned out to be duds? She twisted the bag ties around her fingers. Herbert had reckoned Sam to be a professional, but how did he know? Wasn't it possible the editor could be going on hearsay and had no firsthand knowledge of his skills or otherwise? If she took her camera along she might be doing *The View* a favour, and what a scoop to have *her* photographs featured in the colour supplement!

'Look, I'm just about whacked now,' said Sam, pushing back his sleeve to inspect a large chromium sports watch. 'It's a hell of a long way to fly from Aussie, your arms get tired. I must check in at my hotel and grab some sleep, otherwise I shall topple over. Suppose I come back around clocking-off time and we can go and have a drink somewhere, and work out the timetable for our Paris trip? You'll have had a chance to discuss things with the show business girl by then and you'll know what's involved.'

'I'd rather not have a drink. I prefer to keep business to business hours,' Jenna said in a tight voice.

Sam rested his chin on his chest, looking steadily across at her through thick dark lashes. 'I'll flake out, honeybunch, if I don't get some shuteye, and tomorrow

I'm off to Scotland. I won't be back until a day or two before Viv's film premiere. I'd rather get things sorted out now.' He raised his head. 'It won't take long. One drink and we'll be through.'

Jenna did not know which dismayed her most, the thought of keeping Christopher and Mrs Millet waiting, or the prospect of a drink alone with a man, a man who was tall and tanned and . . .

'No, I can't,' she burst out.

'I'm not going to seduce you!'

He was sharp, too sharp. He had honed on to her sexual drift almost before she had defined it herself.

'I know you're not,' she began indignantly, lamely finishing, 'but I'm going out this evening straight from the office.'

Throwing back his head, he laughed out loud. 'Then why the panic? In that case there's no alternative but to leave the arrangements until I return.' He pushed away his chair. 'Here, I'll give you a hand.'

Before Jenna could stop him, he caught the duffle-bag from her lap and was in the process of swinging it on to his broad shoulder when he stopped. 'Hello!' he said, grinning. 'What's this?'

In fidgeting with the ties she had loosened them and a furry arm was waving to the world.

'A present,' she put in hurriedly, her over-active imagination visualising how Sam would report the bear's existence to Herbert who, in turn, would demand an explanation. Then the editor would learn about Christopher and, now armed with the necessary ammunition, would embark on a campaign to have her dismissed.

Sam pushed the folds of suede aside to drag the bear out into the daylight. 'A present!' He gazed at the single eye, the leg hanging on by only a few stitches, the bare patch on its tummy which Christopher rubbed just before dropping off to sleep. 'Come clean, honeybunch.

Even if there's a market in antique bears, which I doubt, this little fellow isn't about to win any prizes.'

'It belongs to a friend,' she blustered, grabbing the bear from him and ramming it deep into her bag.

'Kinky!' He stood for a moment waiting for more, but Jenna kept her lips shut tight. 'Are you coming?' he asked, seeing she was about to offer no further explanation. He turned towards the door.

'I'll be along in a minute. I need to make a few notes,' she fenced.

'Fine.' He gave a farewell salute and was gone.

Jenna waited until she heard the downward whirr of the lift and then sank back into her chair, lifting a hand to her brow. It was no surprise to discover the skin was burning. Sam Wood was too astute, too direct. Thank goodness he was off up to Scotland! In Paris she would have to be on her guard, otherwise she might let it slip that she was not the childless widow everyone imagined. Jenna took several deep breaths, absentmindedly fingering the crumpled sheet Sam had discarded. She spread it flat and automatically read the words, words in capital letters which he had covered with twirls and flourishes, hearts and flowers. MY DIVINE JENNA, he had written!

# CHAPTER TWO

'EVERY thinking woman must realise the male is an endangered species,' Maggi declared, pouring a liberal splash of white wine. She nodded towards the bottle. 'You're positive you won't?'

'No, thanks.'

Jenna placed a palm across her glass, for her hostess had a nasty habit of topping up regardless in an attempt to bring you level with her intake, which was prodigious.

The *Vogue*-smart brunette pivoted, raising her glass on high in a flourish of declaration. 'Men are as much use to a woman as her appendix—mere remnants left over from the Dark Ages which serve no useful purpose. We're better off without them.' Pronouncement over, she sank on to a bronze velvet chaise-longue, draping herself in a pose reminiscent of a stagey Cleopatra.

'Mmm,' murmured Jenna. She was aware that her function this evening was that of a strictly non-participating audience, though the odd round of applause at Maggi's dramatising would be permitted.

When she had told Sam Wood that she was going out, Jenna had been telling the truth, though her appointment had not been straight from work. Instead she had driven home to her tiny terraced house and to Christopher, who was once again his merry self, showing no sign of damage from the crying jag earlier in the day. Because the evening was cold and wet she had driven Mrs Millet back to her nearby council flat and then returned to make dinner. Afterwards she and Christopher had shared a noisy bathtime, she had

played with him, swapped cuddles, sat him on her knee
while she read a story, produced the requested lullaby,
and by eight o'clock the little boy was tucked up in bed,
fast asleep. Rapidly changing into a petrol-blue velour
jumpsuit, Jenna had brushed her hair, applied a whisk
of mascara, and was ready and waiting when Veronica,
the teenager from next door, arrived to babysit.

Evenings out were rare. Evenings were set aside for
washing and ironing, darning socks, patching dungarees,
writing grocery lists and generally keeping herself one
step ahead. With a covert glance at her hostess, Jenna
wondered why on earth she had elected to spend some of
her precious free time with Maggi of all people. She was a
mere acquaintance and, in truth, Jenna did not like her
very much. But Maggi had lived alone since her husband
had moved in with his secretary a few years ago, and the
bond of being women on their own had pushed Jenna into
accepting the invitation. That, and the suspicion that
behind Maggi's brittleness lurked a lost soul.

Surprisingly it had been Edward who had brought
them together. He had appeared on a television
programme which fell under the brunette's jurisdiction,
and by some curious twist of fate he and Maggi had hit
it off. Social invitations resulted and for a few months
the two couples had met frequently; Jenna and Maggi's
husband always playing second fiddle. Maggi had
lavished praise, describing Edward to everyone as 'the
brilliant Member of Parliament for Altford' and hinting
at Cabinet promotion around the corner, while he had
responded by declaring that she was 'the brightest
producer television has seen in a long time'. The break,
which was inevitable since they were both strongminded
and stubborn, had been bloody. Edward had put
forward one of his pet political observations and Maggi
had felt compelled to disagree. Histrionics on her part
had followed, while he had retreated into his usual
obstinate stance.

'Keep well clear of that self-opinionated shrew,' he had instructed, scoring her name from his address-book. 'She's totally unreasonable, refuses to see any other viewpoint than her own.'

Jenna had almost choked on the irony, for if anyone clung to their own views through thick and thin, it was Edward. If he decreed black was black then it was so, but equally if he decided black was white, then that was not to be questioned either. She had obeyed his order, for Maggi had always been his friend, not hers. But one day, some months after Maggi's husband had departed, she had met the woman accidentally in town and in an uncharacteristic moment the brunette had burst into tears. Jenna had taken her home, offering sympathy. On that occasion all the amateur dramatics had been set aside, for Maggi had spoken honestly of her loneliness and grief. Yet ever since the subject had been taboo, and now an invisible barrier existed which Jenna knew better than try and surmount.

'How's life at the television studios?' she asked, coming back to the present.

'So-so.'

Beanpole-thin, her hostess leaned forward to straighten the hem of her tube dress across her ankles. Of late dieting had become a fetish, and the ankles protruding from the tight skirt were like sticks. Jenna suppressed a wry grin. What an oddity she made in Maggi's fastidious world! She ate heartily and brimmed with good health, and her busy lifestyle left little time to pay undue attention to her appearance. She eyed her chunky black suede boots, comparing them symbolically with the teeter-high satin stilettoes which exactly matched the citrus yellow crêpe-de-chine of Maggi's dress. Her hostess had honed good grooming into an art-form; all her outfits being painstakingly co-ordinated.

Jenna saw she was wearing a set of necklace, ring and

bracelets in topaz and silver, with a matching clip to hold back the ruler-straight fall of dark hair. Eyes travelling further, it was apparent that the elegant chaise-longue teamed exactly with the bronze curtains, and the plain white walls held framed acrylics echoing, once more, the same bronzy shade. Even an exotic Japanese flower arrangement of driftwood and dried thistleheads contained chrysanthemums of bronze and yellow. Citrus yellow, Jenna noticed, coming full circle, a colour which mirrored the shade of Maggi's dress. A mixture of amusement and admiration bubbled through her. She recalled her mismatch of jumpsuit, boots and leather jacket, and promised herself that one day she would go through her entire wardrobe with an eye to reorganisation.

'I was forced to throw a tantrum today,' mused Maggi, downing more wine. 'There was this dreadful man who refused to accept my point of view. I knew I was right, so I screamed a little and he backed down.' She lifted her glass, gazing dull-eyed through the pale yellow-green liquid. 'Men only give pain. I'll never know why you chose to stay with Edward for so long. I swear if he hadn't died you'd be with him yet.'

The slurred comment took Jenna by surprise. On the two or three occasions a year when she and Maggi met, they kept the conversation to generalities. An invisible, yet invincible, line had been drawn and personal matters were avoided.

'Everybody respected Edward,' she said, thrown on to the defensive, for who was Maggi to throw stones? 'He was hardworking and reliable, and . . .'

'So what!' came back the jeer. 'And he was distinguished, with black wavy hair going grey at the temples, very smooth and all that jazz, but . . .' she flung a manicured hand impetuously, 'but he was wrong for you.' The thin terra-cotta lips that complemented her fingernails drooped down and there was a harshness to her tone. 'It's a fallacy that women need men.'

'Not even to unscrew the lid on the marmalade when it's stuck?' Jenna offered with deliberate gaiety, attempting to steer the conversation on to a more flippant, less personal track.

The dark wings of hair swung in a precise negative denial.

'Men are useful for carrying suitcases,' Jenna insisted, her smile bright.

'Buy a trolley.'

'And for checking the oil level in the car and knowing if the tyres are at the correct pressure.'

'Use the service station,' came the humourless reply.

'How about for sex?' she joked.

The wine had loosened her tongue, too, Jenna realised, for the instant the words emerged she regretted them, and it was apparent from Maggi's firming of her lips that the notion was a little too close for comfort.

Her hostess swung from the chaise-longue and walked a trifle unsteadily towards the drinks cabinet. 'Sex is overrated,' she announced, grasping the wine bottle by its neck to replenish her glass. 'And I doubt your Edward was exactly a tiger in bed.'

Round-eyed, Jenna stared at her. In her mind Maggi was picking the wings off a butterfly, and the butterfly was her marriage. 'What do you mean?' she asked, with a sense of impending doom. She did not like to hear her husband's name raised in this way, but was compelled to discover what came next.

'In my business it's wise to check people out. Everything I learned about Edward pointed to the fact that he couldn't possess much of a sex drive. He was forty years old when you married and previously he had always had friendships with women, never affairs.' Maggi took a long pull at her glass. 'Chances are he was a virgin when you became his wife.'

The definition pierced her like the ice-cold point of a dagger.

'If that was true, would it matter?'

'*If?*' The word was pounced on. 'From the expression on your face I'd say there was little doubt.' Jenna averted her eyes and the brunette's tone became world-weary. 'You were very young and innocent. I don't suppose you had a clue what Edward was really like, though you must have discovered later, to your cost.'

'To my cost?' Jenna echoed. The conversation resembled malevolent waves, swelling one by one to drag her from the safety of the shore into murky depths.

'You're a healthy young woman, I expect you enjoy sex. *And* you're attractive to men.'

'I don't—I'm not!' she squeaked, rising impulsively to her feet. 'I'm not interested in that kind of thing. Good heavens, no one has asked me out since——' she searched through her memory, 'since before I was married, and that's nine years ago.' Briefly her mind slid to the tanned Australian, but a drink to discuss business was scarcely a date.

'They won't, if you don't project the right vibes,' her hostess scoffed. 'But in my view you're far better steering clear of the opposite sex, except Christopher. How is the little pet?'

The switch in conversation demanded too wide a leap, and there was a pause as Jenna struggled to assemble her thoughts. She knew Maggi was papering over a gaffe which, had they both had more sense and less wine, would never have arisen. Sex and men and other disturbing images were being pushed firmly away into a dark closet and the key turned.

'He's fine,' she managed to say, and subsided into her chair, gamely gathering up her composure. Talking about her son was balm to her bruised emotions and as she related his progress, some of her tension ebbed.

'Life's never dull with a two-year-old around, though he's nearly three now. He's getting older and so am I—thirty is around the corner!' She groaned in mock despair, rolling her eyes to the ceiling.

'Join the club,' Maggi replied. 'But doesn't he miss not having a father?'

The wine *had* loosened her hostess's tongue this evening, Jenna decided unhappily, for now they were back to men again.

'Not really, what you've never had, you never . . .' Her voice died away, but seconds later her face brightened. 'He's only recently discovered that families generally include fathers. He surprised me this evening when the milkman called and he piped up, "Hello, Milkman-Daddy".' Jenna giggled. 'I didn't know quite what to say, but the milkman thought it was a great joke. He's a grandfather and he reckoned it made him feel young again.' She became pensive. 'I hope Christopher doesn't make a habit of calling strangers "Daddy", it could be embarrassing!'

Conversation drifted on and surreptitiously Jenna kept scanning her watch until, at last, it reached a time when she could decently say farewell. The evening had resurrected too many memories, memories better left alone.

'We must get together again,' Maggi suggested when they were standing in the hallway. 'Let's not leave it so long next time.'

Jenna tugged on her gloves, emerald knitted ones which, she realised, had been taken from the drawer in a hurry and did not match a single thing she was wearing. There was a hole in one of the fingers and she frowned at it. 'I can't arrange anything right now. I'm off to Paris in a couple of weeks.'

'And what's happening over there?' Maggi was beaming foolishly, clinging on to the door for support now that the wine had taken outright control.

'I'm writing a profile on Vivienne Valdis and part of the assignment is to cover the premiere of her latest film.'

'Makes a change from poli ... politics,' Maggi giggled. 'Are you leaving Christopher with Mrs Millet?'

'I hope so.' Jenna pushed her gloves more tightly down between her fingers. 'I'm choosing the right moment to raise the subject, but it's just for a few days and if the worst comes to the worst I can always fly back home. Paris is only an hour away by air.'

If only Christopher was capable of realising how close at hand Paris really was, Jenna thought, pacing through the airport concourse, but when you were two years old and wanted your mummy it made no difference whether one wall, one hour or one thousand miles separated you.

'Don't go, Mummy. Don't go!' he had begged that morning, tears running down his flushed cheeks and dripping off his chin.

Jenna had wiped them with her fingertips as Mrs Millet and her husband watched on anxiously.

'Mummy will be back soon,' she had promised, half wishing she had taken the coward's way out and disappeared without revealing that she would not be around for a few days. But to disappear without warning would be cruel. She was terrified that he could reach the position of not trusting her, never being able to rely on her coming home at the end of the day as promised, so it was vital she be honest—but how her honesty had hurt!

Mrs Millet had agreed to take charge during her absence, though there had been unspoken reservations behind the elderly woman's compliance.

'Why don't you and your husband move in here while I'm away?' Jenna had suggested, hoping to make things easier. Mr Millet had been forced to retire early owing to an asthmatic condition and it was in order to eke out his small pension that his wife looked after Christopher. If they lived in her house they would be using her heat, her electricity, and perhaps that would save them a pound or two.

'Good idea,' the woman had smiled, the lines on her plump face easing with relief. 'It'll be better for Christopher if he's in his own bed.'

Jenna had looked puzzled. 'But he didn't mind staying at your house last time, did he?'

'He did cry a little bit at nights, dearie,' Mrs Millet had admitted, with an uneasy smile.

Jenna's heart had plummeted. There had been no mention of any night-time distress when she had collected him after her absence at the party political conferences. Mrs Millet must have been shielding her, acting from kindly motives but not giving the true picture. How much *did* her son cry when she was away? And now, as she studied the yellow direction boards for the Paris flight, Jenna's stomach was knotted like frozen ropes. She swerved towards a phone booth. What a relief it would be to call and discover that her son had settled happily and was playing with 'Mr Millet-Daddy' as he had taken to calling the old man. But suppose she rang and Christopher was still crying? Oh God! she thought, running a hand across her brow in distress, what do I do then?

'It may never happen,' a melodic baritone said in an unmistakable Australian twang, and she spun round.

'Sam!' she said breathlessly, putting a hand to her throat to stave off the surprise.

He bent his head, examining her expression. 'Are you okay, honeybunch? You look a trifle ... askew.' His dark brown eyes slid over her and there was the lurch of a grin as he surveyed her flying-jacket, blue jeans tucked into shortie suede boots and scrunched-up legwarmers in pale lilac. 'You haven't conformed to Herbert's ideas of fashion yet, I see.'

'Neither have you,' she retaliated, swinging reluctantly from the phone booth.

Sam was also in jeans, they looked new, but the bulky sheepskin jacket was the one he had worn at the meeting, the leather rubbed shiny in places. When he lifted her case she smiled, hurrying to keep pace with his long strides towards the check-in desk. It was only the third time they had met and yet, for Jenna, there existed a double illusion of familiarity and strangeness. His visit to Scotland had been extended and he had only appeared at the office late the previous afternoon to discuss their trip and arrange a rendezvous. When he swung ther cases on to the weighing platform and straightened, the girl behind the counter produced a wide smile.

'Glad to have you with us, sir,' she sparkled, examining their tickets.

Jenna was convinced the different names did not go unnoticed. The receptionist considered Sam was unattached and his manner as he leant on his elbow towards her, resting a lean hip against the counter, confirmed his bachelor status. Jenna hitched her duffle-bag further on to her shoulder and scowled. Okay, so he had a devastating smile. He moved with effortless grace, muscles smoothly oiled, and he was tall and tanned, but so what? Strands of sunbleached hair were straggling over his eyes and he reached up to push them aside, smiling at the girl through his fingers which seemed to turn her heart around and, curiously, Jenna's, too. Grumpily she shifted her weight to the other foot. The only thing Sam Wood had to worry about was where his next admirer was coming from, which was no worry at all, whereas she was churned up with the torment of deserting her infant son. Seconds ticked by and still Sam and the girl were deep in conversation, a conversation spiced with laughter and much female batting of the eyelashes. Jenna realised she would have to accept that he inspired a surfeit of admiration. Doubtless Vivienne Valdis would be all over him too, because from what Shelagh had told her, and the cuttings she had examined, the actress enjoyed a hectic love life.

'All correct.' Sam spun round, giving her scarcely enough time to disguise her irritation at the girl's lush attentions. He hoisted a large leather holdall on to his shoulder. 'All my gear,' he explained, following her glance. 'There must be several thousand pounds' worth of cameras and equipment in here. I daren't let it out of my sight.' He grinned down at her duffle-bag. 'I presume that goes as handbaggage too? You won't want to be parted from your teddy-bear?'

The amusement in his voice dissolved her pique and she grinned. 'I decided to leave it at home for this trip.'

'Good. I expect you prefer to have a far more virile animal than a teddy-bear in bed with you at night!'

The distinctly sexual note made Jenna's cheeks grow pink. Was it because he was Australian, or just because he was himself, that he had such an outspoken approach? He's an unknown quantity, she thought. How different he was from Edward. Her husband had been predictable down to the last comment.

The flight was uneventful and Jenna successfully remained cool and calm throughout, though, at times, her pulse raced a little faster when he was particularly frank. Sam's attitude towards her was wickedly mocking as though he suspected she was unused to the company of a man who said what he liked, when he liked. Despite having spent the last few months in what appeared to be the back of beyond, he was surprisingly au fait with current events and had an intelligent awareness of the British political scene, so the conversation had flowed easily.

'What inspired you to take up political reporting?' he asked when the cab they hailed at Charles de Gaulle airport was speeding along the motorway towards Paris.

'I took economics, history and politics at university,' she began.

'You have a degree?'

Jenna ran her hand beneath the blonde curls, lifting them free from the back of her neck. 'No, I gave up the course in order to be married, but I completed three-quarters of it. Then I married a politician.'

Sam was circling a pattern on the seat between them with an index finger. 'Why didn't you continue your education?'

'Edward asked me to finish. He was a candidate for an important constituency and preferred to have me as his wife rather than a student girl-friend.'

'Good for the image?' Sam commented, and his mouth curled. 'A young blonde bride must have captured quite a few votes.'

Jenna bridled. 'Naturally I worked with my husband on the canvassing, but it was my own choice. I went round from door to door.'

'And still do?' For some reason there was steel in his voice.

'No, not now,' she said. 'I've given up all that kind of thing. It's of no further interest now that my husband . . .'

The words dried as it struck her that Sam imagined she was still married, he could not know Edward was dead. Everyone at the newspaper offices knew she was a widow, but Sam had only been there briefly. She opened her mouth intending to explain, but closed it again. Something made her hesitate. If the Australian realised she was unattached, might he not decide she was therefore available? He had made no secret of his liking for her long legs, supposing he chose to like more? *My* divine Jenna, he had written. It would be characteristic of his freewheeling style for him to try and make her his if he knew she was a widow.

Jenna rammed her hands into her pockets, balling
and unballing her fists. She had had enough of men.
For six years she had been Edward's wife and only fate
had stepped in to free her. Another relationship,
particularly one with a marauding colonial who had the
unhappy knack of throwing her off balance with every
other comment, was no go. *No go!* she told herself,
glaring at him as ferociously as though he had
suggested they strip off their clothes and make love in
the back seat of the taxi. That was exactly the kind of
suggestion he *would* make!

'Don't blame me if your husband's a louse,' Sam
drawled, and she looked hastily away, frantic because
she was exposing more than she meant to. A curious
telepathy appeared to exist, on Sam's side at least, and
when she retorted, 'He's not,' he merely raised his brows
in a way which was too knowing and which did little for
her composure.

'I expect your husband is a fair bit older than you?'
He was moving his finger in ever-decreasing circles over
the strip of leather between them.

'Twenty years.'

'I see.' A muscle clenched in his jaw. 'And what age
are you?'

'Almost thirty,' she mumbled, suspicious of the
conclusions he appeared to be reaching. She could
almost see his brain ticking over—jaded middle-aged
husband, vibrant young wife.

'You and I are in the same age-bracket. I'm thirty-
two,' he said, consciously or unconsciously coupling
them together.

'But we're very different. For instance, you're not
married,' Jenna pointed out hurriedly. It was a foregone
conclusion. She would have also liked to stress that a
bachelor could have no inkling of what fighting for
survival as a single parent could mean, but she blotted
out the temptation.

'I'd like to be married one day,' he said.

Her blue eyes narrowed. 'Would you?'

She had imagined him living life to suit himself, not caring 'tuppence for the trail of broken hearts he must leave behind him, laughing at the girls who longed to tie him down with fetters of matrimony. How could he be sincere in wanting to throw his freedom away? Her independence had been hard won and it was difficult for Jenna to imagine anyone *giving* it away.

Sam shifted, stretching out his legs. 'If I could find a tall blonde with lilac legwarmers and a dimple in her chin, I'd get married tomorrow,' he said, his brown eyes gazing steadily into hers.

As he spoke he raised his index finger and gently dabbed at the cleft in her chin.

Jenna jumped back as though she had been stung and produced a trill of laughter which fooled no one. 'The grass is always greener on the other side of the fence, but thanks for the compliment.' The best strategy must be to pass the comment off as a joke. 'I bet you say that to all the girls!' Okay, she knew it was a hackneyed response, but his touch had been oddly intimate and now her heart was thumping out of tune.

'No, I'm a very straight guy,' he replied, staring down the long length of his denimed legs to his boots. 'I've reached the time in my life when I don't want to go it alone any more. I need an anchor, but the problem is finding one that isn't attached to some other guy's boat. I've left settling down rather too late, and now I'm discovering that the cream of the crop was picked long ago.'

'Perhaps you haven't tried hard enough.'

He grinned lopsidedly. 'You could be right.' Running his fingers through his hair, he bent his head to squint through the windscreen. 'Here we are.'

The newspaper had booked them in at a large modern hotel in Sèvres, a Parisian suburb, and when

the various forms had been completed and the keys
handed over, they took the lift to the twelfth floor.

'Rooms 1204 and 1205,' Sam commented. 'Sounds
like we're next door to each other.'

They were. Sam slung her case on to the bed and
departed, but his proximity was disturbing and try as
she might Jenna was unable to block out her awareness
of him in the next room. There was a connecting door
which she stealthily checked and discovered it was
locked, thank goodness.

'Shall I phone Viv to set up an interview and photo
session?' Sam asked, standing in the corridor smiling at
her when she opened the door to his knock some ten
minutes later. 'She's in residence at some swanky hotel
in the city centre, isn't she?'

Jenna nodded. 'I'd be grateful if you would arrange
things. Hold on a minute, I can give you the telephone
number.'

When she went to find her folder he followed,
slouching a denim hip against the dressing-table as she
rummaged through the sheets of paper. He had
removed his jacket and the grey sweatshirt he wore
outlined the breadth of his chest in a way which made
Jenna's heart quiver. What's the matter with me? she
wondered, writing out the number with shaking fingers.
For years I've never bothered about what men look like
and all of a sudden Sam is haunting me. It must be age,
she decided, thirty must be dangerous. But if she was
overly aware of Sam's physique now, what would she
be like when she was middle-aged? A vision of herself,
grey-haired and bespectacled, drooling over young men
in tight jeans flashed through her mind, and she
grinned. The grin faded. Sam's jeans were tight, his
legs firmly muscled beneath the blue denim. Swallowing
hard, she switched her eyes back up to his face and
glued them there.

'Honeybunch,' he said, shaking his head with wry

amusement, 'if you don't want me to guess what you're thinking you'll have to start wearing a paper bag over your head!'

Jenna flushed scarlet. 'I don't know what you mean,' she replied haughtily.

He put his hands low on his hips and crossed his feet at the ankle. 'You're wondering what I'm like in bed.' His brown eyes were glittering with unholy glee.

'I am *not*!' She was hot and cold all over, her pulses surging with quicksilver and panic.

Grinning, he flexed his shoulders with ostentatious virility and said, 'But you'll never know, honeybunch. What a pity you have to miss out.'

Jenna's mouth flapped open and closed like a freshly caught mackerel. Some pert put-down was needed to keep him firmly in his place, but she could bring no such jibe to mind. Sexual mockery was a new experience. Edward would never have dreamt of speaking in such a manner—but then there had been so many things Edward would never have dreamed of doing.

Thrusting the phone number towards him, she gabbled, 'If you could arrange for me to see Miss Valdis this afternoon that would suit, and perhaps another interview after the premiere to tie up any loose ends?'

He frowned at the slip of paper. 'I'll do my best, but . . .'

'Her agent knows we're in Paris, it's all been set up in advance,' she insisted.

Sam rubbed the back of his neck doubtfully. 'Yes, but Vivienne's a fly character. She'll have you hanging on for days if you let her.'

'I won't,' Jenna said firmly. Four days she would stay at the maximum, and if she had the opportunity to fly back to London earlier, she would.

'You might not have any choice,' he pointed out. 'You're not reporting on politicians who are eager to put across the party manifesto and who work to a strict timetable. These film stars hang much looser. They enjoy keeping the media around, it's a boost for the ego, and makes everyone suspect they're akin to God. We could find ourselves here for longer than anticipated.'

'No, no!' she protested wildly, her anxieties about Christopher tumbling over one another.

'Don't worry. There are worse things in life than being delayed in Paris, even in winter.' He reached out to trail his fingers across the fleecy lapel of her jacket. 'Isn't it about time you took that off?'

'Oh!' Turning, Jenna thrust the jacket hurriedly from her, dropping it on to the bed. She had been too distracted by her unpacking, over-conscious of Sam's movements in the next room, to remember to remove it.

'Your shirt-tail's hanging out,' he said, with a wide grin. 'Turn round.' Before she knew what was happening Sam spun her around by the shoulders so that her back was to him, and tucked her shirt into her trousers with competent fingers. 'There,' he gave her bottom a pat. 'All shipshape and luscious.'

His easy familiarity reminded her of the way she dealt with Christopher, and left her not knowing whether to feel pleased or affronted.

'Does your husband approve of the way you dress?' he asked, strolling over to the window, unaware of the chaos he had created. 'Personally I like your style, but I had the impression politicians' wives were ultra-conventional, decked out in little black dresses and such.'

'I dress to please myself,' she retorted, but could not resist a smile. 'Edward would have a fit if he could see me!'

And how! she thought. Throughout her married life she had conformed. Neatness had been Edward's byword. He had always noticed a scuffmark on her oh-so-sensible court shoes, a pulled thread. Whenever she had rebelled against the conventional clothes, feeling she was being made old and stuffy, he had pointed out that as the wife of a Member of Parliament she had an image to maintain—a respectable image. The voters would not welcome a 'hippy', as he called anyone who failed to subscribe to his sartorial standards. The voters! How she had grown to detest the mythical voters who had controlled her life.

She joined Sam at the window. 'Look, there's the Eiffel Tower!' she exlaimed.

He grinned at her naïve delight. 'You'd never think it's been standing there for nearly a hundred years, would you?' It was a clear cold day and the spires and steeples of Paris stood out in relief against the grey of the winter's sky. Sam named buildings Jenna had only read about in books or seen on television. 'And that's the Seine down there, and to the east . . .'

'You appear to know the city off by heart,' she remarked.

'I've stayed here several times.'

She regarded him afresh. Perhaps he was not entirely the backwoods maverick she had imagined.

'I heard you speaking French to the taxi-driver,' she said, 'and it didn't appear to be of the schoolboy variety.'

He shrugged. 'I get by. I spent a little time in Vietnam and picked up some French there.'

'Vietnam!' Jenna knew she sounded impressed, but she was.

Sam slid a hand beneath his sweatshirt and idly rubbed his midriff. 'I was very young, it was a long time ago. How far have you travelled?'

The rhythmic glide of his hand attracted her attention. What did his skin feel like? Probably it was firm and warm and silky-smooth, teak-brown all over . . . Jenna cut the thought dead and turned instead to stare resolutely out at the Parisian panorama, pulling her mind sternly back to more mundane and ladylike thoughts.

'Er—Blackpool and Brighton are my main haunts,' she confessed. 'That's where the political conferences usually take place. I did go abroad once or twice when I was a teenager, but only to Europe.'

'So you've never roamed any fields larger than a vegetable patch?'

She laughed. 'No. My husband believed—believes,' she corrected, 'in setting a good example by supporting the British tourist industry. Besides which, he hates foreign food.'

'He doesn't know what he's missing.'

Jenna just smiled.

He snapped back to business. 'I'll phone Viv.'

'Call from here,' she offered.

'Thanks.' He sat down on the bed and lifted the receiver, speaking in rapid French. 'I'd like to speak with Miss Valdis, please tell her it's Sam from Sydney,' he said when he was connected. There was a pause and his face darkened. 'No, I'm not prepared to tell you more. Just pass on my name, we're old friends.' Covering the mouthpiece with his hand, he said to Jenna, 'There's some bloody know-all throwing his weight around. Wants me to leave a message and let her ring back. Cheeky bastard!' He waited impatiently, revving himself up for a further skirmish, but there was a trill of a light feminine voice and Jenna saw him relax. 'Hi, Viv, Sam here. Are you still misbehaving yourself?' The reply made him chuckle. 'I've missed you, but give me a break, mate.'

Listening to him, Jenna was abruptly conscious of how Australian he sounded. His relaxed manner made it so easy for her to forget he was a stranger from a distant land who had lived a very different life from hers, and she wondered what it was that made him appear familiar.

'You know I'll always love you, too,' he said into the phone, and gave Jenna such a broad wink that she realised she had been openly studying him.

Embarrassed, she swung to examine the view, but found it impossible to ignore the conversation, so she stood, eyes trained on the grey path of the Seine, ears trained on Sam behind her. His relationship with the actress appeared to date back many years and there was plenty of laughter and teasing comments, but as the phone call wound on Jenna grasped that Vivienne Valdis was not prepared to meet them that day. She began to seethe. Shelagh had given her the impression everything would be straightforward, but already arrangements were threatening to go astray. And to think, she could have been at home now with Christopher instead of kicking her heels on the wrong side of the Channel.

'Well?' she demanded, as soon as he replaced the receiver.

'The day after tomorrow,' he said, spreading his hands in a gesture of resignation.

'The day after tomorrow!'

'She wants to rest this afternoon, and because the premiere's tomorrow she'll be tied up with manicures and having her hair fixed so she'll see us the following day.' He frowned at Jenna's expression. 'Don't get twitchy, it's only a twenty-four-hour delay.'

'Only!' she retorted bitterly.

Sam rose to his feet and strolled over to stand in front of her. 'A day will soon pass. We can do some sightseeing, would you like that, honeybunch?' Without thinking, he stretched out a hand and ran his fingertips along the curve of her cheek. 'It'll be fun, you'll see. I've often wished for the opportunity to take more photos of Paris, and now I can.' Suddenly he jerked his hand away and rammed it into the back pocket of his jeans, moving aside to frown out at the sky. 'Though I wouldn't be surprised if it snowed.'

By mid-afternoon the sky had darkened to lead-grey and when Sam suggested a walk along the river bank Jenna refused, pretending it was far too cold. Cheerfully he accepted her excuse at face value and disappeared, leaving her on edge, worrying about her son and the troublesome delay. She spent a long time stood by the window, but she was blind to the beauty of the scene. The sooner Paris was behind her and she was on her way home, the better.

Sam's forecast came true. By morning Paris had been transformed into a white wonderland, nestling beneath a sparkling quilt of fresh snow. Was the weather identical in London? Jenna wondered, looking out at a sky which was now a deep cobalt blue. Last year Christopher had been too young to romp in the snow, but this year—this year she would build him a snowman and take him sledging in the local park; *if* the snow had not disappeared before she returned home. This morning her spirits were sturdier, for when she had telephoned the previous evening Mrs Millet's assurances that her son was happy had sounded genuine. She was trapped in Paris, so why not enjoy the experience? Now she felt buoyant, Sam no longer posed a threat, and she was happy to fall in with the plans he outlined over breakfast.

'Suppose we visit Notre Dame, Montmartre and the Sacré-Coeur, and . . .'

'Wait, wait, they're all just names to me!'she laughed. 'I don't mind where we go. You're the boss.'

'Fine,' he said, smiling at her with such obvious pleasure that her natural colour intensified and her heart embarked on a private fandango.

What's the matter with me? Jenna asked herself when she went up to her room to dress for the outdoors. She pulled an emerald knitted cap over her blonde curls, a cap which, she realised, *did* match her gloves and

legwarmers. For some strange reason Sam's particular
brand of masculinity had made her vulnerable—too
vulnerable. Grow up, she told herself. He's a carefree
pagan who fascinates you because he's so different from
Edward, that's all.

But *how* different! The blond giant who introduced
her so enthusiastically to Paris was at the opposite end
of the spectrum to her husband. Edward had been
cautious and reserved, acutely conscious of doing
everything in the correct manner. Never, like Sam,
would he have chatted to the man selling hot chestnuts,
or taken photographs for fellow tourists who were
viewing the gargoyles of Notre Dame, or swapped jokes
with the waitress who brought them foaming mugs of
chocolate. Edward would have been incapable of taking
a sensual delight in the crunch of virgin snow beneath
his boots, or pointing out the breathtaking delicacy of a
spider's frozen web. He would never have caught hold
of Jenna's hand and made her run laughing with him
through the park, or showered her with snow from an
overhanging branch, or told her she had cheeks like
rosy apples and please could he have a bite? She had
been throwing a snowball in retaliation when Sam had
taken her photograph, the first of many, as he chased
her through the ankle-deep snow.

'Let me take one of you,' Jenna had panted,
uncovering her camera, and as she had fiddled with the
focus, Sam had quietened and they had spent the next
hour discussing camera techniques. She had listened
intently, picking up valuable tips and had come to
accept that Herbert's words had been accurate; Sam
Wood was a professional.

'You're not such a novice at photography yourself,'
he had grinned as they wandered up through the Jardin
des Tuileries to the Louvre and she snapped some
typically touristy views for her album. How his
comment pleased her!

At sunset they returned to the hotel. Although they had stamped their feet and shaken off most of the snow clinging to their clothes, some stubborn flakes remained. Now they were melting and Jenna's jeans were growing damper by the minute.

'I'm going to strip off and leap into a nice not bath,' she declared, unlocking her bedroom door.

'Can I come too?' Sam teased, but his grin faded abruptly. 'I'm sorry, I mustn't keep saying things like that, must I? They upset you.' Irritably he moved his muscled shoulders beneath the sheepskin jacket. 'They upset me, too. Damn you, Jenna, why do you have to go and be married?'

She stared at him in astonishment. What was he doing? They had only known each other a couple of days and already he was admitting to feelings which were far too intense. But were they intense, or was it merely his devil-may-care attitude that made him talk in this manner?

'Don't look at me like that,' he growled. 'Just because you're married it doesn't mean I can't . . .' He broke off. 'Oh, what the hell!' Roughly he took hold of her arm, pushing her away. 'Go and have your bath.'

Chewing her lip, Jenna went into the room and closed the door behind her. She didn't know what to make of Sam. He couldn't *mean* what he said, could he? No, it was ridiculous. He was just an errant bachelor. Seduction, or whatever it was he was involved in, was second nature. Peeling off her sodden jeans, she hung them to dry on the radiator and shook her head ruefully. If he discovered she was the mother of a chubby two-year-old boy his interest would soon fade. A shadow crossed her face. And if he ever realised her shortcomings as far as matters of love were concerned, he would be off like a shot!

She marched into the bathroom and turned on the taps, leaping for safety when a deluge of hot water shot out from the shower spray above her head.

'French plumbing!' she grumbled, craning beyond the splashing waterfall to fiddle with a confusing array of chromium taps and plungers. She had no wish to take a shower, she wanted a bath, a long hot soak to counteract the January chill. Screwing up her face, she experimented with all the taps in turn, but without success. Only the shower spray produced water and now the jet was near boiling point.

'Sam,' she called, knocking on the connecting door, 'how do I stop the shower and start a bath?'

'Hold on.'

Seconds later he was at her door, striding through to the bathroom. Jenna hastily arranged her sweater over her hips. Barelegged, only her jeans were missing. She was wearing far more than she would have worn on the beach, she told herself, but Sam took no notice of her half-undressed state, frowning as he bent to twist a tap to the left. Miraculously the splash of water ceased.

'You have to turn that one,' he explained, looking up at the shower. 'And then . . :' Without warning the jet shot on again, hitting him full in the face. 'Oh God!' he gasped, burying his head in the towel she pushed hurriedly at him.

'Are you okay?' The water was steaming and Jenna remembered how once Christopher had scalded his hand and how much he had cried.

Sam wiped his face and blinked a couple of times, then he smiled. 'I'm fine, it was just a shock.'

There was a dull red mark on his brow.

'You aren't scalded?'

Jenna raised her hand to push aside the shining fall of sunbleached hair, and felt Sam grow tense beneath her touch. Their eyes met, locked. Time stood still.

'Jenna—oh, Jenna!' he breathed. He hauled her into his arms and his mouth descended.

# CHAPTER THREE

His kiss was hard and demanding, shocking her to the core. Jenna plunged both hands against his chest and wrenched herself free, pressing back against the bathroom wall in a desperate attempt to put as much space as possible between them. She was shaking, her breath a jagged cacophony of shallow gasps.

'No—don't touch me,' she implored. 'Leave me alone!'

Sam gazed down, his brown velvet eyes revealing a surprise as genuine as her own.

'I really didn't mean to...' Roughly he rubbed the thick blond hair at the nape of his neck. 'Honestly, darling, I..' He stopped short, bewildered by the endearment which had sprung unbidden from his lips. He took a deep shuddering breath. 'Jenna, I apologise.' He was formal now, steeling himself to make amends in the correct manner. 'I'm not in the habit of making advances to married women. I never have, I never will. I don't know what came over me. It's just that you and I..' He slammed an angry palm against the tiled wall above her head, leaning over her. 'God! I don't know what it is about you. Perhaps we met in a previous life and that's what makes it seem as though we ought to belong to...' He broke off, shaking his head in tormented confusion.

'Get out,' ordered Jenna in a low vicious tone.

'I'm going.'

'And don't ever, *ever* do that again!' She backed hastily into the bedroom. 'I don't want anything to do with you. We're here for a job of work, that's all.'

'I agree,' he said making for the door. On the

51

threshold he paused. 'If we dine at six that should allow plenty of time to reach the cinema before Vivienne's arrival.'

'I'll eat alone in my room, thank you,' Jenna said primly.

He arched his brows. 'Aren't you overreacting? It was only a kiss. Hardly that, thanks to the speed with which you flung me aside.'

'And what would have happened if I hadn't?' she retorted, then, finding the thought too much to bear, hastily added, 'I don't mess around either. I happen to believe in the sanctity of marriage.'

'Good, that makes two of us.'

'You stick to your part of the assignment and I'll stick to mine,' Jenna glowered. 'There's no reason why we should . . . overlap.'

With a curt nod of agreement, Sam swung from the room, and Jenna sank down on the bed, her mind whirling. What would have happened if she had not had the presence of mind to sheer away from his embrace? Her outrage *had* been too extreme, she knew that, but she was a novice where snatched kisses were concerned. Edward's lovemaking had been in line with his character, written into his timetable by prior arrangement and carried out with a minimum of fuss. Exuberance and impromptu displays of kissing and touching made him uncomfortable. Over the years he had required little in the way of physical affection, so she had learned that her response must be tepid. But Sam would not want a tepid partner, he was young and strong and virile, a sensual man, an earthy man. He would demand more, far more than she was prepared, or able, to give.

In halting French Jenna ordered a meal from room service and later, when she heard Sam's door close and his footsteps fade along the corridor, she telephoned home. The bedroom walls were sturdy, but who knew

what conversation might penetrate through the connecting door? With him safely downstairs in the
restaurant she could relax. When Mrs Millet brought
Christopher to the phone he was cheerful, and she spent
a long time talking to him, closing with a snatch of his
favourite lullaby and a lavish farewell, rich with noisy
kisses. The call must have taken longer than she
imagined, and only minutes later Sam knocked on the
door to advise her it was time to leave.

Much to her surprise, for by now she had sourly
dismissed show business and everyone connected with it
as unreliable, two tickets had arrived from Vivienne
Valdis's publicity agent. They would be watching the
film in style, once Sam had taken the necessary
photographs.

'Isn't this the third so-called premiere?' he enquired
as she climbed ahead of him into the taxi.

Jenna tucked herself neatly into the far corner and
placed her duffle-bag on the seat between them.
Perhaps she was being overly cautious, but from now
on physical contact was to be avoided.

Waiting until Sam had rattled off the instructions to
the driver, she gave a nod of confirmation. 'The studios
came up with the bright idea of a series of premieres in
different countries. The first took place in Hollywood,
the second in Tokyo, and now here.'

'I bet Viv's enjoyed the hoo-ha.'

'Have you known her long?'

'Ages,' he said briefly.

The taxi accelerated and as they neared the city
centre Jenna's interest switched to their surroundings.
'What's that building?' she asked Sam, 'and that?'

Despite his running commentary, the atmosphere was
stilted. He must have reached the conclusion that any
lighthearted banter was risky, and was now intent on
keeping her at arm's length. Thank heavens! she
thought, touching her lips with the back of her hand as

she recalled the alarm which had pulsed through her when his mouth had claimed hers. Alarm, and what else? His kiss had been firm and avid, not like Edward's sparse gestures which had been anaemically soft. Jenna pulled herself up short; comparing Sam and Edward was dangerous.

Sam's commentary faded and they sat in silence, each immersed in their own thoughts, as the taxi travelled along the snow-covered streets. The night sky was dazzlingly clear, with a silver moon and stars twinkling above. Paris was as splendid by night as it had been during the day. Golden beams floodlit the richly-carved palaces and cathedrals, the fountains, the squares with their statues, and now the parks had been turned into black and silver frosted expanses of fairytale woodland.

'Herbert would approve of your outfit this evening. You're the last word in elegance,' Sam told her, his face hidden in the shadows.

Jenna smoothed down the braid edging of her jacket. 'Thank you, I decided to dress up. After all, it's not every day I attend a film premiere.' Her black velvet jacket and trousers were worn over a frilly white silk blouse, Victorian-style, with a high collar. She had pinned an oval cameo at her throat and caught up her hair into a topknot, loose tendrils curling about her ears. To complete her appearance, her chunky boots had been replaced by high strappy black-patent sandals.

'But still with the duffle-bag?' he mocked, smiling down at the bulky wedge between them and then up at her, so that she caught the flash of his teeth in the moonlight.

With a careless laugh, she edged the bag closer. Concealed inside was her camera, but Sam must not know. 'I carry it around by habit.' She eyed the expensive cameras hung around his neck. 'You're pretty loaded up yourself.' There was a pause and then she said casually, 'Where do you intend taking your photographs?'

He grimaced out at the freezing night. 'Inside the foyer, it's far too cold to be hanging around on the pavement. Besides, if I know the French press it'll be like a rugby scrum out there once Viv appears! I reckon I'm better off stationed indoors. She's scheduled to greet a line of dignitaries in the foyer, so there'll be ample opportunity for photographs there. You go and find our seats and I'll join you later.'

'How many photo sessions do you intend to have?'

'I don't know. Initially I intend to play it by ear, so I'll come along with you to the interviews and wait for inspiration.'

Behind her polite smile of acceptance, Jenna's mind worked overtime. She had entertained the half-formed idea of asking Vivienne Valdis to pose for her when Sam was firmly out of the way, but now it seemed he could stay too close for comfort. *And* he and the actress were friends, so perhaps she might not agree to Jenna muscling in on the action. Tonight must be the night! A series of action shots of the actress's arrival at the theatre, stepping from her limousine, caught with a smile for the cheering crowds, would surely attract Herbert's attention. And should *The View* decide not to use them, perhaps she could sell her work elsewhere. She would be making another stride towards her independence. In this world a woman on her own had to fight for her share of the spoils, and all thoughts that her intentions might be unethical were thrust aside as Jenna dreamed of the end result. Once she was an established freelance she would be able to devote far more time to Christopher. He would be happier and so would she. Sam had only himself to worry about, so if some of her photographs happened to be used in place of his, that was just hard luck!

Fans were already gathered on the pavement when the taxi dropped them off in the Champs Elysées, and Jenna tucked herself firmly in behind the tall Australian as he engineered a path through the throng.

'Off you go,' he said when they reached the crowded foyer. 'I'll see you later.'

Obediently she followed the shallow carpeted steps towards the circle, but at the top of the staircase she swerved aside and headed for a door marked '*Dames*'. The room was empty and Jenna rapidly unpacked and adjusted her camera, checking the flash. When she was satisfied, she hoisted her duffle-bag on to her shoulder and made her way to the head of the staircase. Below her the foyer was a mass of people, all talking and laughing, and she had to search for a glimpse of Sam. His height and fair hair revealed him in a far corner, engrossed in conversation with another man, his back to the melée.

Stealthily Jenna made her way down the stairs, against the oncoming tide of cinema-goers, while she kept a watchful eye on his broad outline. His companion was speaking earnestly, flinging out his arms in Gallic windmills and absorbing Sam's complete attention. When she reached the porch she gave a huge sigh of relief and slid out into the cold. The temperature was below freezing and her breath misted white on the air. Within seconds she was shivering, for her jacket was little protection, but Jenna tucked her collar around her neck and convinced herself that it would all be worthwhile.

Where the snow had been shovelled aside, a red carpet stretched from the short flight of steps at the theatre's entrance down to the kerb and halfway along were a gaggle of pressmen, chattering amongst themselves. When she approached, one of them, a cheery type with a droopy handlebar moustache, winked. He spouted a mouthful of French which had her smiling inanely and holding out her press card in mute explanation.

'Ah!' he said, rolling his eyes.

He muttered something to his companions, prompting

eyebrows to be raised, shoulders shrugged, but seconds later she was forgotten.

Jenna's toes grew numb in her high-heeled sandals, and she stamped her feet and jiggled around in an effort to keep warm. Behind the barriers the fans were growing restless. They, too, were rubbing their arms and blowing on their fingers, but all thoughts of the bitter cold receded when, way up the hill towards the Arc de Triomphe, a cavalcade appeared, led by a huge black Mercedes with headlamps blazing.

In a trice the crush of photographers doubled. Men with cameras rushed out from nooks and crannies where they had been keeping warm, though Jenna noted with relief that Sam was not among them. Now she was surrounded, jostled on all sides. Adrenaline surged through her veins as she fought for a position near the kerb, holding her camera steady with both hands. Someone kicked her shins, but she stood firm. The leading car drew to a halt. There was a moment of incredible tension when the crowd held its breath, then a uniformed commissionaire stepped forward to pull wide the door and there was a collective sigh of delight as Vivienne Valdis surfaced from dark leather depths to accept the adulation.

Jenna pushed aside an arm which was blocking her view and began to snap briskly—one, two, three. The actress was moving slowly, thank goodness, for now the wad of photographers had been joined by a television crew and it was all Jenna could do to maintain her position. When an elbow jutted to shove her aside, she shoved back. It was dog eat dog.

'*Merde*!' someone expostulated behind her.

The following limousines drew up in turn, disgorging the actress's entourage. Jenna recognised a plump Arab who dabbled his financial fingers in the cinema world, a film director of yesteryear, but most of the faces meant nothing. On the off-chance that they were newsworthy, she continued snapping. The film was an Anglo-French production with a large cast, and presumably the men in tuxedos and the decorated females were supporting players.

As Vivienne Valdis and company undulated along the red carpet Jenna found herself carried along in the midst of a bedlam of pushing, shoving, cursing men. She was squashed, her arms pinned to her sides, and taking pictures proved impossible. A television interviewer, all smiles, held out a microphone and the actress paused to speak. Jenna caught her breath. No longer peering down the aperture of a viewfinder, she could now see Vivienne in the flesh—and what flesh! It was milky-white and smooth as buffed satin. She had thought herself thinly dressed for the arctic temperature, but the redhead was wearing only a wisp; a tight-fitting petunia-pink metallic sheath which hung precariously from diamanté straps to reveal swells of bosom, a curved spine almost down to the realms of indecency and tantalising glimpses of thigh through strategically-sited slits. Jenna knew now why the actress had needed a whole day to prepare herself, but equally accepted that she was being churlish. The woman was a natural beauty with large green eyes and flaming hair, but the spiky false lashes, the teased sunburst of gleaming tresses, the lace ostrich-trimmed cape billowing around her, added a theatrical dimension that separated her from everyday life. The crowd had come to see glamour and Vivienne was giving full value.

The sheath dress clung and moulded, making it outrageously apparent that underwear did not feature in Miss Valdis's scheme of things. Several photographers were murmuring observations, both flattering and lewd. As the television interviewer continued his questions, Jenna noticed a thin young man with black hair and goatee beard who was hovering close to the star. Like the other men in her party, he was wearing a white tuxedo, but a pair of dark glasses concealed his eyes, projecting a distinctly menacing air. Jenna shivered. This must be the creepy publicist Shelagh had mentioned and who had prompted Sam's wrath over the telephone. It was obvious that the actress's replies to the interviewer had been rehearsed, and once the publicist's fingers bit into her elbow, making her pause and rephrase her answer. Jenna could not decide whether the resultant look Vivienne threw at him was wary or scornful, maybe it was a little of both.

The woman was a man-catcher, of that there was no doubt, for as she bestowed her smiles, male eyes glazed and mouths gaped. When Sam had told Vivienne he loved her perhaps he had not been joking. Every other man appeared to fall headlong beneath her spell, why not him?

The interviewer departed. Shouting requests and instructions, the press mob swept like a runaway truck towards the theatre steps, carrying Jenna in its midst. The *force de frappe* slammed away her breath and she clung desperately to her camera, dipping and bobbing to manoeuvre a better-position. A gap appeared. She took one shot and then another. Photographers swirled around, but Jenna kept snapping wildly. On reaching the short flight of steps, Vivienne Valdis swivelled on the crest, throwing out her arms in a final I-love-you-all gesture to the shouting fans. Jenna felt a sharp blow in the back of her knees and twisted to glare briefly at a small thug of a man behind her. He did it again. She winced. Good God, he was doing it on purpose! He was hacking her down like a sapling in order to commandeer her position. Another blow hit the soft sensitive joint. Jenna tensed her legs, she would not give way, she would *not*!

There was a sudden mob rush, the man shouldered forward, pushing her off course, and the spiky heel of her sandal caught between two paving slabs and

snapped. She stumbled, her knees buckling, and began
to collapse. Everything happened in slow motion as she
toppled backwards, clawing for support. But each
sleeve she plucked at was jerked free, and she was
ruthlessly hurled aside, poleaxing to the ground with a
vicious thud. Stars danced before her eyes, jitter-yellow
and crimson, and then everything went black.

Her head was throbbing. Jenna lay very still, eyelids
opening cautiously as her hands crept up to examine the
damage. Dimly she recognised that she was back at the
hotel, in bed, and pale light was filtering through the
curtains. When she discovered a lump on the back of
her head, she moaned. The swelling was the size of
a ping-pong ball—painful, fiery and infinitely tender.
She whimpered and as she recalled the wretchedness of
the previous evening, tears squeezed through her lids
and trickled down her cheeks in self-pity. She sent all
continental photographers winging off into hell. Often
she had come across television crews and press at
political meetings where everyone was boisterous,
urging M.P.s to give a quotable comment, but never
had she encountered such brutal disregard. There was a
handkerchief beneath her pillow, and as she blew her
nose Jenna grew calmer. How had she returned to the
hotel? Vaguely she remembered being lifted from the
ground. There had been a car ride and what then?
Surely a doctor, a man reeking of hair oil who had
given her an injection and presumably tucked her up in
bed.

   'Good morning, how are you feeling?'
   Sam came in through the connecting door which
was now open wide and without waiting for a reply
strode to the window to wrench the curtains apart.
White morning light flooded in, making Jenna shield
her eyes.

'My head hurts,' she complained.

'I'm not surprised.'

The coldness of his tone made her blink and as she adjusted to the glare she saw that he was stood at the end of her bed, arms folded in a gesture of disapproval.

'Last night was horrible,' she whined. 'I always believed Frenchmen were gallant!'

'Spare me the tears.' He threw a withering frown at her damp cheeks. 'You got all you deserved.' He gave a hiss of impatience. 'I must be the world's greatest fool. I honestly believed you were decent and honest. You didn't appear to hide a thing, it was all there to read in those big beautiful eyes of yours. Lady, how wrong I was!' He took a step forward and Jenna hastily pulled the sheet up to her chin, cowering behind it. 'You're a devious bitch, Jenna Devine! But don't imagine I shall be duped again.'

'I was only taking a few photographs.'

'Without telling me?' He gave a bark of sardonic laughter. 'I can read between the lines. You kept mighty quiet about your intention to sneak out to the kerbside. What was your game? Did you intend to supersede me at *The View*, or are you in league with some other publication?'

Jenna gulped. His face was rigid with anger, a nerve throbbing irritably in his temple.

'It was practice.'

'Practice! Who the hell practises with a rabble like that? You were out to take saleable shots. I've come across women like you before—greedy little cows who want it all for themselves. The fact that my part of the assignment is to take the photographs didn't trouble you one bit, did it?' He glared at her. 'You, I remember, said we weren't to overlap, but you just went and crawled all over me!'

Her comment about overlapping had applied more to their personal relationship than the working one, but

Jenna sensed it would be downright suicidal to raise
that point while he was stood above her, nostrils flared
in rage.

'I know now exactly where I stand,' Sam announced,
shooting her a warning glance which killed her hastily
summoned protestations stone dead. 'From now on you
can play this assignment your way and I'll play it mine.
You report *and* take photographs and so will I! I've
written articles before. You're as new to the entertain-
ment world as I am, so there's no reason why I
shouldn't stand a damn good chance of coming up
trumps. At the end of the day we'll both submit our
work to Herbert and let him decide which he accepts.'

Jenna's spine prickled, then there was a huge rush of
terror. Herbert would be bound to accept Sam's work
because Sam was male.

'No, I don't want to do that,' she gasped. 'Look, I'll
give you my film.' She swung her legs out of bed, but
then swung them back in again when she realised she
was wearing her semi-sheer baby doll pyjamas.

'Keep your film!' he snapped explosively, paying no
attention as she scurried back beneath the sheets. 'You
can finish the reel this morning. If you remember, we're
due at Viv's hotel in less than an hour's time.' He
paused and added scathingly, '*If* you feel fit enough to
attend. If not, then I guess I shall be going alone.'

'I'm okay, it's just that the bump is tender.' She
fingered it carefully. 'But I'm in working order.' She
smiled, trying to turn it into a jest.

'I thought you might be,' he sneered, but he sighed
and dropped down on to the end of the bed, relaxing a
little.

Jenna watched, wondering if this could be the first
sign of Sam relenting. She was wrong.

'Tell me something,' he growled, the brown eyes
disdainful. 'You're married to a prosperous politician,
you must earn a healthy salary yourself, and yet you

still want more, at my expense! Why can't you be
satisfied? I have to make a living too, you know.' His
tone remained harsh, his face still taut.

Deciding she did not wish to be trampled underfoot,
Jenna pushed herself on to the pillow, wrapping the
misty-pink coverlet under her armpits, like an Egyptian
mummy. 'I want to be a freelance, a photo-journalist,'
she explained.

'Why?'

'In order to be independent, so that I can choose my
own hours and not be under anyone's thumb.'

'And work more closely with your husband on the
political scene?' he probed.

*'Oh no!'*

Sam ignored the consternation which had opened
wide her blue eyes. 'You have to be damn good to make
a living from freelance work.' He shot her a look that
indicated he was doubtful of her ability.

'If I can improve my photography I should be fine,'
Jenna said. 'I've done all my sums, I know I can exist
independently, given the right breaks.'

'What is it you want to be independent of?' he
demanded, his eyes keen. '*The View* or your husband?'

Jenna's fingers curled around the edge of the coverlet.
'I don't know what you mean,' she stalled, avoiding a
direct answer.

'You've been on pins ever since we arrived. You
admitted there was some kind of trouble in the
background.' The muscles in his neck tightened
involuntarily. 'I overheard you blowing kisses down
the telephone. Who were you speaking to—a lover?'

A splutter of nervous laughter burst from Jenna's
lips. 'A lover? Good heavens, no! That was my . . . my
nephew, Christopher, he's two years old. The teddy in
my duffle-bag belonged to him,' she added for good
measure.

At the news Sam sagged somewhat, so Jenna

produced a winning smile and began to make elaborate amends. 'I had no intention of taking over your job. I merely thought an additional shot or two outside the cinema might be worthwhile.'

'But supposing I'd decided to install myself out there?'

His question foiled her deceit, but she kept the smile pinned firmly on to her lips.

'We could have pooled our resources.'

'I bet!' He was angry again. 'I suppose you had it all planned how you'd gang up with Vivienne against me and take a secret set of photographs?' He gave a bark of disgust. 'You picked the wrong girl when you picked Viv. To put it bluntly, she and I are like this.' He crossed two fingers and thrust them under her nose. 'And that's me on top, lady, exactly where Viv prefers me to be. If you were expecting it to be a case of feminists of the world unite, then allow me to enlighten you. Viv likes men. She realises male and female can have much more fun making love, not war.'

Jenna examined the coverlet. 'I'm not out to strike blows for femininity,' she protested, giving him a hurried glance, but Sam's grim expression showed he was not prepared to allow her an inch. He was forcing her to capitulate. 'I'll give you the film,' she offered again. 'And I promise not to take any further shots of Vivienne Valdis.' A spark of defiance made her enquire, somewhat tartly. 'Will that do?'

'It *sounds* fine, but you're at it again, looking as though butter wouldn't melt in your mouth. Don't forget I know that behind those cornflower-blue eyes of yours lives the soul of Dracula.' He gave a scornful laugh. 'Don't go making any promises just in case you have to break them.'

Her chin shot up belligerently. 'I have no intention of breaking them. I give you my word I won't take any more photographs unless I have your permission.'

'I'm hardly likely to give that, am I?' he drawled, then rose to examine his watch. 'If you want a bite of breakfast before we leave, I suggest you get a move on.'

'I will, as soon as you're out of the room,' she retorted. Friendship was impossible, judging from Sam's tone, so she decided to follow his lead and restrict herself to scarcely concealed hostility.

There was an enigmatic look and one brow twitched. 'You're too late for modesty. It's sure as hell not going to inflame my passions if I see you getting out of your pyjamas, considering I put you *into* them.'

Jenna's hand flew to her throat in dismay. 'You did what!'

'For God's sake, don't look so mortified. You're a married woman, a man has set eyes on your unclothed body before, I presume?'

'But—but I thought there was a doctor,' she replied lamely, ignoring the mockery behind his comment.

'There was.' Sam pursed his lips. 'Don't you remember what happened last night?'

'Not clearly. I remember cracking my head, but the rest is vague,' she confessed.

'Well, for your enlightenment, when I was taking up my position to photograph Viv in the foyer there was one hell of a commotion. Some guy rushed in yelling for an ambulance because a girl photographer had passed out. I investigated and found you, spreadeagled on the ground.' His tongue clicked in exasperation. 'There was a great deal of Gallic excitement, ooh-la-la's, arms flying, talk of whisking you off to hospital, but it was clear you were only dazed and had no broken bones, so I loaded you into a taxi and brought you back. I reckoned Herbert wouldn't relish having to cough up for your medical bills!' he added pithily.

'So you didn't take any photographs of Vivienne?'

He frowned. 'How could I? When we arrived here I asked the receptionist to call a doctor, just to be on the safe side. He came and confirmed that you were all in one piece. The diagnosis was slight concussion and that you'd be fine after a good night's sleep. He gave you an injection to calm you.'

'Why didn't *he* put me to bed?' she demanded hotly.

Sam rested his hands on his hips, glaring at her with bleak impatience. 'Because, honeybunch, he was a suave type who made me cringe. His hair was coated in grease and he was awash with some hideous aftershave that made him smell like a cross between a Norwegian pine forest and a field of carnations. And when he looked at you he forgot he was a doctor first, and a man second.'

'And aren't you a man!'

'Yes, but I'm not a lecher.' He shifted irritably. 'Stop looking so outraged—I've seen naked women before.'

'I suppose you have,' she muttered. In the silence that followed Jenna decided she was being ungracious. 'Thank you for ... for rescuing me. I'm sorry you missed out on your photographs.' A thought struck her and her face brightened. 'Perhaps we could use ...'

'Don't you dare say it,' he cut in savagely. 'There's no way your photographs will appear alongside mine.' He strode towards the connecting door. 'Now, hurry up, and don't worry, I shan't be sneaking a peep through the crack. I have better things to do!'

Sunk in the depths of a squashy scarlet brocade couch, Jenna tried hard to ignore her throbbing head. The interview was proving far more elusive than she had ever imagined and Vivienne Valdis had disappeared into the bedroom yet again, this time to answer the telephone. The publicity agent, eyes obscured by the ominous dark glasses, was vigilantly placed between the actress in the bedroom and Jenna in the lounge, while Sam slouched by the window, gazing at the snowy streets.

After a rapid shower, hasty mouthfuls of too-hot coffee and a nail-biting drive, they had arrived at Miss Valdis's luxury suite with minutes to spare. Jenna was the one who had been rapid, scalded and frantic. Sam, by contrast, was the ultimate in relaxation, becoming calmer and more lazily self-possessed by the minute. He was, she realised, a man who had come to acceptable terms with himself, and the knowledge annoyed her intensely. What did *he* know of life? He didn't have to contend daily with biting remarks from a disapproving tyrant like Herbert Holt. His job was not perpetually hanging by a thread—if, indeed, he troubled with regular employment. Probably he worked only when he needed ready cash. Jenna had not asked about his background because, she told herself, she did not care. In any case, becoming too inquisitive might bounce back on her and lead to trouble.

Ever since she joined *The View* she had deliberately refrained from making close friends, terrified they might discover she had a child and reveal the fact to Herbert Holt. In the past the editor had had trouble with mothers who had put their children before the newspaper's interest, and now he was adamant that he would employ no more women with family ties.

'Why ask for trouble?' he had said, reasonably enough but cutting too near the bone for her peace of mind. 'Women with children, especially small children, are a risk. They're tugged two ways and the family invariably wins. The only reason I accept you,' she had scowled at that, 'is that you're a widow with no attachments.'

If he only knew!

She swung an impatient foot. All that panic to arrive on time and now they had been here three hours, of which only ten minutes had proved productive. Tem minutes when Vivienne had sent the publicist—Josh, he was called—out to buy cigarettes. Ten minutes when she had answered Jenna's questions fairly and squarely. Then Josh had returned, scowling at the tape recorder as if he dreaded what had been revealed during his absence. It was back to the big star protocol with guarded replies and a petulant exchange between him and his charge, which ended with him suggesting a break for photographs.

Vivienne had disappeared into the bedroom, emerging a quarter of an hour later energetically dressed in short flounces of black taffeta, a bolero and thigh-high patent boots. Embarking on a flirtation with Sam and his camera, she kicked up her legs, offered her bee-stung lips for kisses, oozed voluptuously in and out of positions and then abruptly decided her duty was done. The role was abandoned. Now she was the girl next door, hanging on to Sam's arm, demanding news of old friends, recalling long-gone evenings, laughing over their mutual past. Josh and Jenna were excluded, a situation neither of them enjoyed—Josh because the actress was beyond his control, and Jenna because she objected to Sam's smiles and reminiscences. He was wasting valuable time, that was what infuriated her. Josh broke up the intimacy with a hint that a second change of outfit was necessary. Heaving an impatient sigh, Vivienne did as she was told and made for the bedroom.

There was a further interminable wait. She emerged a cowgirl in fringed suede mini and ten-gallon hat. More photographs, more chat with Sam until Jenna had glared pointedly at her watch and he had brought the photo session to an end. Vivienne went again, coming out twenty minutes later in a crystal-pink tabard and tight trousers, eyes made up in rainbow shades of violet and purple with black kohl in heavy evidence and the inevitable false lashes. Now, Jenna presumed, the actress was herself again and the interview could proceed. Hastily she switched on her tape recorder, but the telephone had rung...

In the bedroom Vivienne was chattering carelessly, giving peals of laughter, and it seemed her visitors had been forgotten. Jenna gazed around the sumptuous lounge. Christened 'The Oriental Suite', the actress's accommodation was grand, though Jenna scornfully felt there was more than a passing resemblance to a Chinese brothel. Not that she had ever been to China, or inside a brothel, for heaven's sake, but the curtains of gold organza, the fat scarlet chairs, the mirrors, the black lacquered screens inlaid with mother-of-pearl, were *too* much. A glimpse through the open bedroom door revealed a lofty four-poster hung with scarlet brocade and lace, ideal for entertaining Chinese mandarins or dark-eyed Arabian princes.

She signed noisily, hoping to secure a response from Sam, for surely he was aware of how time was slipping away. No reaction. He seemed content to examine the view, a slight frown indicating that he was engrossed in thoughts of his own.

'Sorry about the delay, folks,' said Vivienne, tripping gaily back. She plopped herself down on the couch. 'Now, where were we?'

Jenna jabbed at the black button. 'Can you give me any reactions to the type of movies you made at the start of your career?' Out of the corner of her eye she saw Josh sidle closer. 'Were they a deliberate ploy to get yourself noticed?'

'Don't answer that,' the publicist ordered.

'And why not?' Vivienne snarled right back, and they were scrapping again.

Sam walked over. 'Why the hell can't you leave Viv to deal with the interview herself?' he asked Josh. 'She's a perfectly literate and lucid woman.'

'She could be misrepresented,' he glowered.

'I have no intention of "misrepresenting" her,' Jenna inserted. 'This is a serious interview. I want to shelve the Hollywood flimflam and write about the *real*

Vivienne Valdis, a woman of our time.' She flung him a waspish glance. 'With your permission.'

In all honesty Jenna doubted there was a *real* Vivienne Valdis; the painted creature beside her resembled a cardboard cut-out of a film star as far as she was concerned. Yet her words seemed to strike home, for the actress's eyes clouded.

'That's a new angle. I'll consider it over lunch,' she said thoughtfully. 'I'd like to break free of the mould, and now could be the perfect opportunity.'

'What do you mean?' asked Josh cagily.

Vivienne shrugged. 'I don't know yet.' She flounced away to smile up at Sam. 'What do you fancy to eat, big boy? Hot, cold, French, Chinese, roast beef and Yorkshire pudding?'

Jenna saw the time drifting by. 'I don't think we need anything,' she cut in, giving a swift hopeful glance in Sam's direction.

'Of course we do—I'm hungry,' he replied. 'We must keep up our strength. How's your head?'

'Fine.'

A band of pain was tightening across her brow, but she was afraid that if she hinted at feeling unwell Sam or Josh, or both, might bring the interview to a close. Having no alternative, she accepted the prospect of lunch with as much grace as she could muster, but grew edgy when it became apparent that the meal was destined to occupy a full hour. Sam and Vivienne chatted, seemingly unaware that both Jenna and Josh were on tenterhooks. As Jenna ate her salad she gave Sam a suspicious questioning glance. Had he abandoned his threat of writing a parallel article? This morning he had not taken any written notes, but his knowledge of the actress and her background was extensive, and possibly the present dialogue was being stored away in his mind for use at a later date. She heaved a sigh of relief when he terminated the conversation, decreeing it was time to resume the interview, *her* interview! Grudgingly Jenna admitted to herself that the meal had been reviving, for her headache had lessened, and now she was impatient to start again.

The publicist positioned himself crosslegged on the floor, only four feet from Vivienne, the shadowy hawk-like eyes alert to every nuance.

'Josh, darling!' the actress exclaimed, sweeping her fingertips to her lipsticked mouth in a gesture of sudden remembrance. 'Would you mind awfully if I asked you to buy me some more of that special cleansing milk? My supply is finished and you know how important it is that I use the correct formula on my skin. The milk is made in France, so it should be easy to find.' She became pensive. 'Or you could call at the manufacturer's own salon.'

'Where's that?' he asked suspiciously, and when she quoted some far-flung suburb he frowned. 'But that'll take hours!'

'Nonsense! You'll be there and back in no time.'

With effusive thanks she hustled him out of the suite before he had time to work out a resistance, and when the door had closed she danced back into the lounge and clung on to Sam, laughing uproariously.

'Thank goodness he's gone!'

'I don't know how you stand him,' Sam remarked. 'He's like Big Brother, constantly spying on you. You don't need him, Viv.'

The actress sucked at a fingernail. 'Perhaps not, but I've always had a man around and . . .'

'Men aren't the be-all and end-all,' Jenna inserted tartly.

'Gee, thanks,' mocked Sam, leaving Vivienne to walk over to her. 'You're great for my morale. Now I feel a good two feet tall!'

'Men help,' Vivienne said wistfully.

Once again the telephone gave its clarion call. The

actress excused herself and disappeared, Sam returned to the window, and Jenna was back where she started, frowning down at the silent tape recorder and swinging an irritated foot. How could Sam remain even-tempered when the whole day was being frittered away?

He turned as if sensing her look and a wry smile quirked his mouth. 'Getting impatient, honeybunch?'

Jenna scowled at the bedroom door. 'Why must it be so long-drawn out?' she complained in a low voice. 'Politicians are far more reliable. They're too busy to waste hours on one interview. If Vivienne doesn't hurry up we shall have to return tomorrow.'

Sam stretched languidly and came to sit beside her on the couch. 'You'd better prepare yourself for a delay. All this behaviour is called feeding the ego, and you're not exactly helping.'

'Me?' Her brows shot to her hairline.

He grinned. 'That Josh guy doesn't trust you an inch—and with reason. You treat Vivienne like a contemporary, an ordinary woman, and it's a new experience. Vivienne hasn't decided yet how to react, and that's what is making Josh uptight. Half of Viv expects you to kow-tow and speak in reverent tones, goggle a bit, pay compliments, say "ooh" and "ah" when she name-drops.' His eyes shone with amusement. 'But the other half finds your no-nonsense approach refreshing. She's deduced that you're not impressed by the clouds of publicity and she's tempted to say "get lost" to Josh and talk freely.'

'Some hopes!'

'But there's an added complication. She's not immune to the fact that if you were decked out in all her finery you'd look every bit as spectacular.'

Glancing down at her plaid shirt and leather trousers, Jenna burst out laughing. 'Sam! I'm not a glossy production.'

'Only because you choose not to be,' he replied

solemnly, lifting a hand to twirl a strand of her hair around his finger. 'You're blonde, she's auburn-haired, but apart from that . . .' He shrugged. 'You both have beautiful skin, high cheekbones, and whoever designed the chassis did a wonderful job.'

When Jenna smiled back into his eyes the inches that separated them seemed to melt away. Sam was absorbing her, his expression gravely tender. A rush of panic dilated her nerves and she frowned, knowing it was wiser to veer from his dark brown gaze, but his proximity on the couch was sapping her strength. Enveloped by his nearness, she was acutely aware of herself as a woman, a desirable woman. The image frightened her. Could it be true? There seemed little doubt Sam was attracted to her, and the longer they were in each other's company the more she felt an urge to respond. It was as though a magnet was pulling them together and she was unable to resist its force. His eyes roamed her face to linger on her mouth, a full mouth, the soft pink lips made for kissing.

'You're beautiful,' Sam murmured as their heads moved closer.

A shriek of laughter from the next room shattered the spell and while Jenna blinked herself back to reality, Sam untangled his fingers from her hair. Abruptly he rose and stood before her, legs firmly apart, his hands pushed into the back pockets of his jeans.

'Do you want to talk?' he asked.

'Talk?' She was puzzled, groping for poise after the moment's searing intensity. 'What about?'

He sighed. 'About your . . . troubles. Look, I know something has gone wrong in your life, and often the best remedy is to talk things over. It clarifies the problem, puts it into perspective.'

Now that he had moved away Jenna felt more sure of herself. 'You're imagining things,' she said coolly.

Sam raked back his hair in rough exasperation.

'Okay, have it your way. All I'm trying to put over i that if you ever need a shoulder to cry on, then I'm here. The world can be a cold hard place when you're out there alone. If you want a friend, you can count on me.'

She cultivated a mask of blasé indifference. 'Stop jumping to conclusions—my life is fine.'

'At least pay me the compliment of being honest,' he growled. 'You're like a cat on a hot tin roof. You hardly ever relax. What you need is a lusty man to cherish you, to make love to you and ...' When he broke off midstream she could do nothing but stare at him in horror. He straightened his shoulders, the anger falling from him like a cloak. 'I'm sorry if the truth is unpalatable, but that's the way it strikes me. That husband of yours isn't doing a very good job o keeping you happy.'

'You're wrong,' she protested, but the grim disbelie tightening his jaw made her add, 'Perhaps I'm a bi tense because I'm away from home.'

'Rubbish! You're a mature woman, so don't pretend two days in Paris makes you homesick. Good grief most people would give their eyeteeth for a trip here, al expenses paid!'

'I'm not most people,' she retorted.

Sam's eyes narrowed and the world stopped turning as he watched her. Jenna felt as though he coul penetrate her very soul.

'What makes you tick, honeybunch? One minute you're looking at me as though you've never seen a mar before, and the next you're so damn nervous you'd cry "rape" if I laid a finger on you.' He sat down beside her, reaching out to clasp her hands tightly in his. 'I want to help,' he insisted.

'Now then, you two, behave yourselves!' a teasing voice sang from the bedroom door. Arms akimbo Vivienne was tapping her foot, delight dancing all over her. She wagged a comic finger. 'So you indulge in tête-à-têtes while my back's turned! I didn't realise . . .'

'There's nothing to realise,' said Sam in clipped tones, rising to stride to the window. 'Jenna and I were talking, that's all. Now let's cut out the pussyfooting, Viv, and get on with the interview. Don't waste any more time.'

The actress clapped a hand to her shiny-moist mouth. 'Am I wasting time?'

'You damn well are!'

'Don't get mad at me because I caught you red-handed,' she coaxed.

Sam looked fierce. 'Cut it out, Viv!'

Jenna picked up her notepad and began thumbing through the pages in brisk determination. 'Shall we get back to the questions?'

The actress threw Sam a wary glance. 'Actually I was wondering if we could finish. I didn't get to bed until four, and if I'm to dazzle this evening an hour or two's rest is vital.'

Sam frowned. 'You realise we've wasted the entire day? The fact that Jenna and I are here to *work* doesn't seem to have entered your head.'

Vivienne looked genuinely dejected. 'I'm sorry—tomorrow I promise I'll stop all my phone calls to concentrate on the interview.' She smiled hopefully across at Jenna. 'Is that okay?'

Jenna nodded her thanks.

'And I don't want to see that publicist guy here tomorrow,' Sam snarled.

Recovering her sparkle, Vivienne pranced to him. 'Don't be cross, lover-boy. This evening I'd like you and your lady,' she glanced at Jenna, 'to have dinner with me, and then we'll all go on to a disco.'

'No, thank you.' His reply was firm.

The actress's finger wagged. 'Aha! The two of you want to be alone together at your hotel. I understand.'

'No, you don't,' he retorted, irritation grinding his brows together. 'Mrs Devine and I are in Paris on a business assignment—period!'

'I'm married,' Jenna said impulsively as though the fact proved something, but Vivienne was worldly-wise.

Her underlip protruded. 'And since when did that make any difference?'

'It does to us,' slammed back Sam.

The woman's lashes fluttered. 'My word, aren't we squeaky-clean!' The fury on Sam's face quelled any further taunt and Vivienne was forced to hurriedly think again. 'Perhaps there's nothing between you,' she conceded, 'but that doesn't mean you can't both be my guests. It'll be fun.'

His mouth twisted. 'Oh yes? And who else is going, all that gang who were in attendance last night?' Vivienne nodded. 'Then no, thank you.'

Jenna knew he was including her in his refusal, but instead of feeling annoyed at the blithe confidence with which he had harnessed them together, she was relieved. Disco-dancing had not been Edward's scene, she was lamentably out of practice. In any case, her head still throbbed and, like Sam, she was chary of Vivienne's companions.

'I have to write up my notes,' she said to strengthen his case.

The actress's mind was elsewhere. 'What's wrong with my friends?' she demanded peevishly.

A faint smile came to Sam's lips. 'Friends? Don't make me laugh! Half of them are hangers-on, all they want from you is reflected glory, an opportunity to have their pictures in the newspapers. They'd kill their own grandmothers if it meant they'd appear in *Le Figaro* tomorrow.'

Vivienne placed her hands on her hips in chagrin. 'And the other half?' she demanded.

'Opportunists—guys who hope to garner some

pickings from your success. I thought you were smart,
Viv, you must realise what sharks these people are.
Take that dreadful Josh. I bet you pay through the nose
for him, and what does he do? Buy cigarettes and
squeeze all chance of any spontaneity out of your life.'

'Sam old Sam!' the actress complained. 'The truth at
any cost. Okay, I agree most of my . . . my friends could
slink away if my next film proves to be a flop, but
they're all I have.'

'And they're all you'll ever get so long as you allow
them to latch on to you. Anyone half decent will take one
look at those types and keep well away. You don't need
them, Viv,' he ground out. 'Or your sex-bomb image. It's
becoming dated and it's self-destructive. Rumour has it
you're developing into a damned fine actress.'

Vivienne's eyes lit up. 'What did you think of the film
last night?'

'We . . . er . . . we didn't manage to see it,' Jenna
confessed hurriedly. 'I . . . I fainted outside the cinema
and Sam had to play Sir Galahad, so I'm afraid we
missed the performance.'

'But you must go.' Her smile swung between the two
of them. 'It's good, *I'm* good.'

'Then for heaven's sake stand on your own two feet.
You don't need the phoney acolytes,' Sam insisted.
'There are plenty of decent people in the film world, so
why surround yourself with the dregs? Abandon the
superficiality, find the confidence to be yourself.'

Vivienne nibbled thoughtfully at a lacquered nail.
'Perhaps you're right.'

'I am.' Sam acted as though he had inside
information on the difference between right and wrong,
and Jenna discovered she was impressed. 'Cut loose
from the bloodsuckers,' he ordered. 'Join the real
people again.'

'Then perhaps I could meet a nice ordinary guy and
get married,' Vivienne mused.

Jenna's blue eyes grew wide in surprise. The cuttings file she had scrutinised had shown a couple of live-in lovers, and a crocodile of temporary men passing through the redhead's life.

'Do you want to get married?' she asked. First Sam and now Vivienne were showing a yen for matrimony that amazed her.

'Doesn't every girl? But I never met anyone suitable.' As if suspecting it was a frail argument, Vivienne added, 'The men I date are professional playboys, insecure actors and such. Not exactly the type to swear undying love.'

'But marriage is very restricting. It's not all fun,' Jenna heard herself saying. When she saw Sam's expression harden, she added quickly, 'A woman has to sacrifice her independence when she marries.'

'I wouldn't mind that,' the actress murmured.

'But Jenna is keen on independence,' Sam inserted.

She darted him a glance, unable to determine just how serious he was being, for his brow had lifted when he sensed her inspection.

'I'm looking forward to seeing your film,' Jenna blustered, squirming free from a conversation which could trap her if she was not careful.

'Why not go this evening? I have some free trickets,' Vivienne smiled as she turned towards the bedroom. 'Hold on a minute and I'll get them.'

# CHAPTER FOUR

INITIALLY Jenna greeted the prospect of an excursion to the cinema with dismay. All she wanted to do was lie down in some dark haven and nurse her throbbing head. However, once the stuffy central-heated atmosphere of Vivienne's apartment had been left behind the fresh air began to revive her, and gradually her headache receded. An hour later the only reminder of her inelegant crash to the ground was a slightly tender lump at the back of her head.

In the event the film proved to be a godsend. It filled the evening and helped to take her mind off Christopher and what could be happening at home. When she had made her usual call, keeping her voice low in order that Sam wouldn't overhear, Mrs Millet had reported that the little boy had gone to bed. At the time Jenna accepted this reason for him not coming to the phone, but later her imagination had leapt into frenzied action. Suppose, if instead of sleeping, Christopher had been too distressed to speak with her? Harrowing scenes flipped through her mind, and by the time Sam knocked on her door and they went down to find a taxi, she had convinced herself all was doom and despair. For some reason Sam was subdued, so Jenna found herself chattering inanely in an attempt to fill the silence and stem her troubled thoughts. What a relief it was when the opening titles rolled and she was able to absorb herself in the life on the screen.

After capturing a major award at Cannes, the film was now breaking box office records, and Jenna soon realised its success was undoubtedly due to Vivienne's skilful performance in the leading role. She exhibited a surprising talent, displaying a wide range of emotions, everything from terror to a low-key wit. Her acting had an integrity that breathed real life into the character, and Jenna was full of admiration, and bewilderment.

'She's far better than I realised,' Sam remarked afterwards, and they both agreed that the sexpot image was totally at odds with the sensitive portrayal they had seen on the screen.

By the time she knocked at the double doors of the Oriental Suite the next morning, Jenna was bubbling with enthusiasm. No longer did she feel halfhearted about approaching a subject she had considered superficial, now her interest had been aroused and she was eager to restart the interview, this time from a completely fresh angle. Vivienne was a complex character and it would be a challenge to pin that complexity to paper.

The actress answered the door, smiling a welcome. 'Where's Sam?' she asked, poking her head out into the corridor.

'He'll be along later, he had some work he needs to complete.'

Quite unexpectedly Jenna's own words hit her hard and her step faltered. Work! What work could Sam have? At breakfast when he had explained he would be tied up for a couple of hours and she must go without him, she had imagined him to be occupied with his photography. Now that seemed doubtful. There were darkrooms at *The View*'s London offices, so it was pointless for him to bother about technicalities while he was abroad. Her brow puckered. Sam's only work must be drafting his article on Vivienne! He was no fool. Indeed, the more she knew of him the more she realised he was far from the modern-day cavalier whistling his way through life that she had first imagined. He would be eminently capable of structuring an in-depth view of the actress—a male view which might well appeal to Herbert. Jenna's temper sparked. He knew she had taken no further photographs and was thus keeping her side of the bargain, yet he was going ahead with his article. Whatever Maggi might say, there was no likelihood of men becoming extinct while predatory specimens like Sam Wood prowled the globe!

'I've been considering Sam's ideas,' Vivienne told her when they were seated in the scarlet and gold lounge. 'His values make sense.'

'Oh yes?' Her reply was noncommittal. Right now she was in the wrong frame of mind to lavish approval on anything *he* had instigated.

'I took a long cool look at my—my associates last night, and I realise it would be no loss to part company from most of them. As a result I've given Josh his marching orders.'

Surprised by the actress's swift reaction, Jenna sat back. 'How did he take it?'

'Not well. The news prompted him to impart what he considered to be a few home truths.' A shadow crossed Vivienne's face.

'Was he nasty?' Jenna shuddered at the memory of those beady eyes lurking behind the dark glasses.

Vivienne took a ragged breath. 'Yes, I'm still picking up the pieces. He was . . . vitriolic. Mind you, at least I know now that I'm better off without him.'

And I'd be better off without Sam, Jenna decided.

Tucking her legs beneath her, the actress curled up in the corner of the couch. 'So the first step towards changing my lifestyle has been taken. From now on the image I project will be the real me.' She patted her cheek. 'See, no make-up!' Stripped of the false eyelashes, the black lines, layers of powder and paint, Vivienne had a delicate beauty. This morning she was dressed simply in a pale apricot blouse and skirt, her hair hanging loose and straight to her shoulders. There was little trace of the vigorously defined glamour-puss of yesterday. She fidgeted with a buttoned cuff. 'I would like to tell the public that all the razzamatazz was a result of my own innocence and stupidity,' she added, 'but that, at heart, I'm a normal intelligent woman.'

'Then I may be able to help.' Jenna whipped through her notebook until she came to the jottings she had made on her return from the cinema the previous evening. 'My intention is to write a warts-and-all account of what constitutes an actress. I want to know your aspirations, your doubts, those insecurities that plague everyone, how you react to the extravagant praise, how you keep sane.' She subjected the redhead to a fierce look. 'If it's going to work you'll have to be honest with me—and I mean *really* honest—then, in turn, I can be honest with the readers.'

'And if, while you're with me over the next few weeks, I'm foolish, or vain, or downright bad-tempered, you'll record it?'

'Yes.'

Vivienne looked down at the hands interlaced in her lap and after a moment she nodded. 'Then let's get the show on the road!'

For two solid hours Jenna plied her questions, and as the time unfolded she had to rework many of the preconceptions she had gained from her research.

'My childhood was comfortable in a material sense, but disjointed because my father was, and is, a diplomat,' Vivienne explained. 'His career meant my life was broken into three-year segments when he moved from one posting to the next. I attended schools in four different countries and later went to university in Australia, that's where I first met Sam.'

Jenna was unable to resist sidetracking. 'Sam went to university?' The image of him as a conventional student, with the discipline of work and examinations to pass, was difficult to accept.

'We were in the same year.'

Jenna frowned, remembering the facts at her fingertips. 'But you're several years younger than Sam, so how come you were students together?'

'Actually I'm thirty-two, not twenty-six as my publicity handout reads. Actresses often subtract a few years,' Vivienne added, fidgeting with her cuff again.

'Do you intend to continue with the deceit?'

The woman's spine straightened. 'Deceit is rather a strong word. It's a white lie.'

Jenna shrugged. 'Okay, white lie.'

'Can you give me time to think about that? Six extra years is rather a hefty amount for the public to handle all of a sudden—and for *me* to handle!'

Jenna gave a chuckle. 'Don't worry, I've reached the age when I feel I ought to start going backwards myself.'

'Though perhaps it would be wise to volunteer the information,' the actress mused. 'Anyone who knows me from the past could let the cat out of the bag any time, and it would be rather humiliating to be forced into confessing my real age. I'd rather give it of my own free will.' She wrinkled her nose, deep in thought.

Jenna picked up the thread of conversation. 'So you and Sam were at university together?'

'He was only there for a year.'

'Then he was booted out?'

'Good heavens, no! He left of his own free will, cut loose and disappeared. Nineteen was a disaster area as far as Sam was concerned, because his mother took ill and died very suddenly, and within months his father remarried. The new wife was only a few years older than Sam and his sisters; a glamorous fashion model. Sam was disgusted by his father's choice of bride and rebelled—but I guess you know all this, working for *The View*?'

Jenna frowned. 'No.' Did Vivienne assume that

because she and Sam were involved in the same
assignment they had delved into each other's background?

'Being an only son, Sam had had a close relationship
with his mother,' the redhead continued. 'Perhaps he
could have accepted a comfortable woman of his
father's own generation as a stepmother, but the notion
of a young fashion plate stepping into his mother's
shoes, and his father's bed, was abhorrent to him.'

'But why did he leave university?'

'Australia suddenly became too confining to contain
both Sam and his father. There was one hell of a bust-
up, and you know how outspoken he can be?'

Jenna nodded, all too aware of his knack of
unsettling her with his unfettered use of the truth.

'He told his father exactly what he thought of him
and his bride, no punches pulled, and then he went
walkabout.'

'Walkabout?' Jenna's winged brows pulled together.

'He disappeared without trace and two years later
flew back home with a collection of photographs of
Vietnam and the boat people. Being Sam, he never went
into details, but I gather he'd lived rough. There were
rumours he had risked his life to help families escape
the country. In due course his photographs were
published and won instant acclaim, receiving all sorts of
awards. I guess his escapades set the pattern for his life
from then on.' Vivienne pulled tautly at her cuff. 'That
was about the time I met Gavrick.'

Jenna was torn two ways. She was tempted to learn
more about Sam's activities but, after all, she was here
expressly to discuss Vivienne's life.

'Gavrick Seymour, your manager?'

'My *ex*-manager,' the redhead said heavily, rising to
her feet. 'Before we start that sordid tale let's have some
coffee.'

They were finishing a second cup apiece when Sam

arrived. He brought a rush of wintry air into the apartment, flicking flakes of white from his jacket, because it was snowing again. He was big and energetic, an outdoors man with his rumpled hair and glowing skin. Depositing two plastic carrier bags on the floor, he began unbuttoning his sheepskin coat.

'I've been shopping,' he explained in answer to the curious glances. 'My nieces and nephews grumble like mad if I return empty-handed from my travels, so this time I've decided to cover myself in glory.'

'Aren't typhoid and bullet holes the standard souvenirs from the countries you usually visit?' Vivienne teased.

He grinned. 'True. Paris makes a welcome change, though I still find myself leaping for cover when a car backfires.' He noticed Jenna's frown. 'Under the misapprehension it's gunshots,' he added.

'Oh,' she said, floundering.

He rubbed his hands together. 'Have I missed much?'

Warning bells rang in her head. 'Haven't you brought your camera?'

Sam collapsed into an armchair, sprawling one long leg over the padded arm and refusing the offer of coffee. 'I'm not taking any photographs today.' He smiled at Vivienne. 'I notice you've left off the goo and got rid of that Josh character, thank goodness. I suggest we revamp your image, add some depth. I'd like to show you learning your lines or working out in the gym.'

'Sounds great, and already Jenna is re-vamping with words.'

'Why have you come?' Jenna was unable to resist asking.

He spread his hands. 'To be with the two most beautiful girls in Paris, and listen in to the interview.'

At last, the truth! she thought. No longer was he

pretending to confine his interest to photography, he had come to take notes, albeit mental notes. Doubtless he had now roughed out his article and knew precisely which line he intended to pursue.

'Don't let me inhibit you in any way,' he drawled, and was rewarded with a scathing glance.

Aware of her disapproval and caring not one jot, Sam leant back in his chair, stretching his arms indolently, the wide shoulders rippling beneath the navy polo-necked jersey.

Jenna frowned. How could she topple his plans? 'You'll find it terribly boring.' A petulant note tinged her words.

'Viv's life boring? You're doing her a disservice,' he teased. 'Besides, if you discover any gaps in your notes at a later date I shall be able to give you the benefit of my knowledge.'

'I have my tape recorder,' she replied, feeling she was being outargued in some sneaky masculine fashion. Half turning her back, she tried, in vain, to ignore the sprawl of his legs in the denim jeans, the idle way he was stroking his jaw as though weighing her up and deciding he had the better of her. She concentrated on Vivienne. 'You were telling me about Gavrick Seymour,' she said in a tight voice.

The actress ran the tip of her tongue over her unvarnished mouth. 'Believe it or not, until I joined forces with Gavrick I was your typical dutiful daughter, very strictly raised, and a girl who conformed. I'd never strayed from the straight and narrow, but I met him and . . .' she shrugged expressively, 'and suddenly I found myself in the fast lane.'

'What kind of a man was he?' Jenna asked.

'He was a good bit older than me. He'd been around and knew the score. I'd never come across anyone in my sphere who was so strong-minded, so definite.'

'Where did you meet him?'

'At an Embassy party in Sydney. He was out there with a touring company from England. The tour had been successful, but it wasn't enough for Gavrick. He'd reached the conclusion that the one way to make the cash register ring was to market smut—and then I walked into his life.' There was silence. A pulse throbbed pale blue in Vivienne's throat. 'He needed a good-looking girl with a touch of class. A girl who could be persuaded to shed her clothes, and her inhibitions, in front of the camera.'

'You didn't object?' Jenna queried.

Vivienne's laugh contained no humour. 'No. He was a smooth talker, a strong personality. Within days we were lovers, and he took control of me from then on, body and soul. Gavrick was the first man I'd ever fallen for, and I was in the seventh heaven. He turned my notions of right and wrong upside down and inside out. Whatever he asked me to do, I did.'

'And he managed your career for several years?'

'Yes. I relied on him right from the start, and before long he was running my life for me. That suited me fine. Occasionally I would resist some distasteful aspect of my career, but he always explained away my doubts. He could coax me into the most incredible situations. I realise I was immature, and my knowledge of life had been . . . conventional. Gavrick was like a tornado sweeping over me.'

'How did your family react to the sex films?'

She groaned. 'They were baffled by this sudden leap from respectability to outright degradation. My mother resorted to tears and impassioned pleas, while my father tried hard to retain some dignity. That was difficult, when anyone could walk into a cinema and watch his daughter romping around in the raw!'

'Didn't you realise you were being exploited?' queried Jenna.

'Deep down I must have done, but I worshipped

Gavrick. I became as skilled at twisting the truth as he was. I used to say things like, quote "I only undress if it's necessary to the plot" unquote. Rubbish! The plots were written to titillate.'

'Why did you break with him?'

'Ironically, because my over-exposure suffered from over-exposure. Once a voyeur has seen a girl naked several times his palate becomes jaded. Someone new is required. Gavrick knew my popularity wouldn't last for ever and he began to look around for a replacement. I didn't know how to react. I loved him, and now I began to hate him. He met an ebony beauty with an inflated bosom, and decided she was his next meal ticket.'

'I've heard of her,' Jenna murmured. 'So what happened when you parted company?'

'For two years I was suicidal. I lived on pills. I missed Gavrick like mad, and I would have taken him back, even then. Also I had a dreadful reputation to live down, and the only scripts I received were more of the "strip off your clothes" variety. There was no future in that.' The pointed chin lifted. 'Gradually I began to pull myself together. I hawked around from one audition to the next, and finally managed to secure a tiny role in a straight film. It was like manna from heaven! I was living on the breadline, because Gavrick had creamed off most of the money I'd earned while I was with him. After the cameo role I was offered a slightly bigger part and people began to realise I was more than a string of measurements.' Her tentative smile grew wider. 'And now this latest film seems to have convinced everyone I'm worthy of serious consideration.'

Sam was leaning forward listening intently, his hands clasped between his knees. '*If* you use your common sense and don't fritter their goodwill away. For God's sake, take a long hard look at yourself.'

Vivienne gave him a mock salute. 'Yes, sir!'

'I mean it.'

'Yes, sir!' she chirped again.

There were more questions, more detailed answers. Sandwiches appeared at lunchtime, but Jenna's tape recorder continued to turn. By mid-afternoon Vivienne was talked out.

'Thanks very much.' Wearily Jenna switched off the machine. She was exhausted too, her mind bursting with phrases, evocative statements, but there had been too much to absorb all at once. It would take time for Vivienne's story to gel. 'The stuff you've given me today will form the basis of my article.' She tapped her head. 'I have the bare bones already arranged up here. I'll put them down on paper and add the flesh as I see more of you over the next couple of weeks.'

She began to pack away her gear into her duffle-bag, now eager to leave. There was nothing further to do in Paris and home was beckoning.

Vivienne frowned at her activity. 'Don't rush away—stay and spend the evening with me.'

Jenna glanced outside at the sky which was sombre with snowclouds. Plans were forming in her head. 'I'm afraid I can't.' She threw a look at Sam. 'Why don't you stay?'

It was an empty gesture. Sam made his own decisions. He would do whatever *he* wanted to do, even to the extent of interrogating Vivienne to discover what he had missed first thing that morning. To her surprise, he shook his head.

'I'm sorry, I must take a rain check, Viv. But I promise we'll go out on the town when we meet up again.'

Vivienne smiled happily. 'Discoing at the Wild Cockatoo, two weeks today?'

He nodded. 'It's a date!'

Jenna turned her key. 'Do you think the planes will still be flying?' she asked, pushing wide her bedroom door.

On their journey back to the hotel the snow had been intermittent, merely flurries in the wind, but the gloomy sky held a threat of heavier falls to come.

'I imagine so, weather conditions aren't that bad, but why?' Sam shifted his carrier bags to grasp the two in one hand. 'You're not intending to rush back to England this evening, are you? Why not wait until tomorrow?'

'I've finished my interviewing for the moment and ... and it looks like more snow,' she blustered, trying to frame her reply not to resemble the frantic getaway it really was. 'What's the point in hanging on here?' When she saw Sam's frown deepen, she added, '*You* don't have to leave. Stay in Paris, take Vivienne to the Folies Bergère or something.'

'Thank you,' he said with heavy sarcasm, following her into the room. 'Why is it I have the feeling you don't want me around?'

She avoided his direct brown eyes. 'I want to get home to Christopher,' she muttered.

'Christopher!' Sam sounded incredulous. He dropped the carrier bags down on to the bed and put a finger beneath her chin, tilting it upwards until she was forced to meet his piercing gaze. 'Are you sure he's only your nephew?'

Jenna flushed. 'Of course I'm sure,' she said with as much conviction as she could find.

'I hope you're telling me the truth.' He groped into one of his bags. 'I was in a toy shop this morning and I bought this. If Christopher turns out to be a husky macho-man of thirty-five he's not going to be too thrilled.'

Curious, she took the brightly wrapped parcel he was offering and tore away the paper. 'A new teddy-bear!' she exclaimed. 'He'll love it.' He would, too. The soft pile was lush, a pale honey colour, silky to the fingertips, and the plump body was perfect for cuddling when you were tucked up in bed at night. Her delight made her smile up at him, her face alive with happiness. She put her fingers on his arm and squeezed. 'Thanks, you're very kind.' Then she caught her lower lip between sharp white teeth. She had forgotten that in reality Sam was little more than an acquaintance. Receiving gifts from strangers was a delicate business. 'But please, let me pay...' she began.

The remainder of her sentence was lost beneath his bellow.

'Let you pay!' he interrupted, incensed with a fury as harsh as it was unexpected. It was all Jenna could do not to cower back beneath the abrupt attack. 'What are you?' he snarled. 'One of those people who can't bear to be...' he chose the word carefully, 'beholden!' He glared at the toy in her hands. 'It's a simple gift, not some kind of bribe. I don't expect any favours in return.'

She felt a pang of regret. She hadn't meant to offend him, perhaps the bang on her head the previous evening had dulled her senses. She would have been more attuned to his personality than to throw the gift back into his face. Whatever Sam was, he was straightforward. He had bought the toy only because he believed Christopher would enjoy it. Chastened, she stepped from him.

'Thank you very much, Christopher will be delighted.' She caressed the furry tummy with her thumb, feeling the springy pile. 'He likes to rub his teddy-bear when he's dropping off to sleep,' she said, trying to smooth over her faux pas. 'It gives him comfort.'

Sam turned aside for a moment and when he turned back he seemed to accept her words as the intended apology.

'It's often the simple pleasures which are the best,' he smiled. 'The sun's heat between your shoulderblades, the breeze in your hair, the smell of newmown hay.' He caught and held her eyes. 'Making love. The glide of skin against skin . . .'

'Stop it!' she pleaded, terrified of what he might say next. She knew he was talking like that on purpose, deliberately arousing a sensation which she had learned to suppress so many years ago.

'Anyone would imagine you were a virgin,' he mocked. 'Or are you a prude?'

'I'm neither,' she returned stiffly. She swung towards the telephone, then halted. 'Please could you ring the airport for me and discover if there's a London plane in about an hour's time? Your French is far superior to mine.'

He clicked his heels. 'Yes, ma'am.'

There was no hassle. Sam reserved two seats by phone and when they boarded the plane it was half empty. Indeed, the airport had been deserted, presumably because all sensible people had cast a discerning eye at the leaden sky and decided to stay home. But soon she would be home, home with Christopher. Jenna sank back into her seat and gave a contented smile as the jet powered along the runway and up into the clouds.

'I presume you intend to give Vivienne a look at your article before it's printed?' Sam asked, scanning the pages of an airline magazine.

She watched him through her lashes. 'No, why?'

'It's one thing to chatter ad-lib, but it's another to see your confessions written down in black and white. When she reads the plain truth she might well have second thoughts. Perhaps she'll decide the "showing-myself-as-I-really-am" angle is too risky.'

'And where does that leave me?' Jenna demanded, thrown on to the alert. 'She can't change her mind midway.'

He was deep in the study of an advertisement for a gleaming sports car. Typical, Jenna thought moodily, the perfect accessory for a bachelor with no responsibilities. She could imagine him hightailing around, the wind flicking his hair across his brow, his hands competent on the wheel, a laughing girl beside him.

'Viv can and Viv might, only *might*,' he stressed when he managed to tear his eyes away from the advertising blurb and contemplate her strained expression. 'You must give her time to accept the idea of being ... meaningful.' He rolled out the word in lazy amusement. 'Don't forget she swapped over images pretty rashly. Maybe she'll decide to swap back when the reality of what she's committing herself to sinks in. You never know, perhaps Josh will reappear bearing roses and boxes of chocolates, and sweet-talk himself back into favour.' Jenna caught her breath audibly, making him pause. He stroked a finger across the back of her hand. 'Don't look so panic-stricken, honeybunch. Equally it could be that Viv was ripe for a change, and you and I were the catalyst which prompted her decision.' His finger moved back and forth, outlining the silky ridge of a bone. 'But she's obviously suggestible, so beware. Remember how she reacted to that Gavrick Seymour, she sounds to have done whatever he asked.'

'I can understand that,' Jenna blurted out, remembering the early days of her marriage.

His finger stopped on her hand. 'Can you? I can't.'

'She was young and immature. It's difficult for a girl to think straight if she's overwhelmed by some man who's much older, and who has his own definite ideas.'

'So in the same situation you would have embarked on a career of stripping naked in public!'

'No.' She found herself grinning with him. 'But I can sympathise. If you've been strictly reared, schooled to behave, then there's a tendency to obey your elders, come what may. It seems natural to accept that they know best. By the time you've gained some maturity it can be too late to extricate yourself from a situation. It's all a matter of innocence.'

Sam leant forward to tuck his magazine into the seat pocket. 'Do I detect a note of worldly-wise experience?'

Immediately Jenna clammed up, her mind racing. What power did Sam possess which induced her to skip rashly to the brink of danger? For almost a year her private life had remained incommunicado as far as her office colleagues were concerned. She had never allowed a casual remark to slip through in case it might lead to trouble, and yet in a matter of days this tall Australian had probed further than anyone had before. And it wasn't as though he had to work hard to secure her indiscretions, indeed she almost *offered* information . . .

She shook her head, managing a little laugh. 'I have an over-active imagination, that's all.'

'Ditto. I said you and Vivienne were interchangeable as far as beauty was concerned, and I keep wondering what you'd look like in the regulation black satin suspender belt and fishnet stockings.' The expression in his eyes made up in full for the immobility of his face.

'No bra?' Jenna queried, but her voice cracked, which rather spoilt the effect of casual enquiry which she had been aiming for.

The look in his eyes was unnerving. Surely her temperature was beginning to rise?

'No bra,' he confirmed gently, and when his eyes fell the tips of her breasts hardened into erotic pebbles.

The idea that he could be exciting her merely by talking froze her motionless. She was being cut in two. Part of her wanted to be able to relax and share his teasing, sexual though it was, yet the other part knew she was too vulnerable. How could she, of all people, cope with a sensual animal like Sam? She pressed a hand to her breast, though whether it was to stave off the fear that gripped her, or to shield her burgeoning curves from his view, she had no idea. She took a deep breath.

'Do you do much disco-dancing?'

He laughed at her oh-so-obvious switch of conversation. 'Not much, but Viv's a great girl for the bumps and grinds. A trip to the Wild Cockatoo will please her.'

'Is it in Soho?' she asked, wrinkling her nose as she tried to place the name. She was not au fait with nightclubs, though they were sometimes discussed at the office.

'It's in Sydney.'

She was perplexed. 'Sydney, Australia?'

'As far as I'm aware there isn't a Wild Cockatoo disco in Sydney, Nova Scotia,' he said drily.

'But Vivienne arranged to meet you there in two weeks' time!'

He shifted slantwise in his seat, facing her. 'That's right.'

'But I'm supposed to be covering her activities...' Jenna broke off, biting her lip. 'If she's in Australia, how can I be with...' The wary expression on his face was enough. '*I'm* expected to visit Australia too!' she shrieked in horror, and when the couple in front turned round to discover who was yelling, she lowered her voice and hissed fiercely, 'This is some devious trick of Herbert Holt's, isn't it?'

Sam wafted a hand in rueful apology. 'You weren't supposed to hear about the next stage of the itinerary until you returned to the office. There's a fourth film premiere in Sydney.'

'And you knew about it!' she accused, her voice rising again. She glared at him, her eyes throwing daggers. 'My God, as far as deceit goes you're in a class of your own! I thought you were my... my friend, but all the time you were in cahoots with Herbert!' She jammed her lips into a hard straight line. 'Well, *I'm* not being coerced into flying to damned Australia, and that's final!'

'What's wrong with Australia?' Sam demanded, his eyes glittering his annoyance at her resistance to visiting his homeland. 'It's a wonderful country.' He scowled out at the wintry night. 'The climate's warm, the natives are friendly and there's plenty of space to stretch your legs. Did you realise that if you drive from Sydney to Perth, the equivalent distance from London would land you in Leningrad?' His lip curled derisively. 'And in Australia they serve *cold* beer! Talk about whingeing Poms, you get top marks! By your own admission you're a stay-at-home girl, and yet you dare to run down another country, *my* country, when you know damn all about it!' His anger swelled as he spoke.

'It's not Australia as such that I object to,' she said hurriedly in an attempt to calm him down. 'It's just that it's . . . it's so far away.'

'I'm so sorry, madam, we'll have it towed up and moored in the Thames estuary,' he said with heavy sarcasm. 'We can't put you to the trouble of a long flight, can we?' He raked an impatient hand through his hair. 'In the name of my career I've slept in hovels, trekked for days through mountains, once I spent over seventeen hours on the deck of a cargo boat taking me from Cyprus to West Beirut. There was no food or drink, and the temperature was over a hundred degrees. And yet you throw a fit about the prospect of a day's flight on a comfortable jet with all mod cons!' He turned away in disgust.

'I don't object to the flight,' she said lamely.

'Then what the hell *do* you object to?'

Jenna was trapped. 'I can't leave Christopher,' she mumbled, her head pounding with inner conflict.

His gaze hardened fractionally. 'You can't leave your nephew?'

'He's not my nephew.' She paused, biting her lip. 'He's my son!'

If she had expected Sam to throw up his hands in

horror, she was wrong. His response was low-key in the extreme.

'So what's your problem?'

'But nobody at *The View* knows about him,' she wailed. 'If Herbert discovered I had a child he would have a strong case for terminating my employment. Company policy is against working mothers. The only reason he accepts me on his payroll is that he imagines I have no ties.'

'But you'll only be in Australia for about ten days . . .'

'Ten days!' She was shrieking again.

'Honeybunch, I realise that your little boy will miss you, but he has *two* parents,' Sam said gently, pressing her hands between his. 'Your husband can take charge.'

'No, no, he can't!' Jenna was seized with panic. 'And if I refuse to go to Australia Herbert could fire me on the spot.' Her eyes were brimming with tears. 'What would I do then?'

Sam was sticking to his own remedy. 'As you and your husband both have careers, there must be give and take. So just make him understand that on this occasion he'll have to help out.'

'That's impossible.' She was staring at him, wide-eyed with consternation. Why on earth had she concocted this foolish lie about Edward's existence? She took a deep breath. 'My husband divides his time between the Houses of Parliament in London and his constituency near Manchester, so it's not practical for him to supervise a small child.' There! that sounds reasonable, she decided.

Sam squeezed her fingers. 'It's not my place to pass judgments,' he began.

Her stomach plunged. 'But you're going to?'

He nodded, rubbing his thumb across her wrist in gentle abstraction. 'If your husband is happy for you to work, and he shares in the benefits your salary must provide, then on occasions he has to make sacrifices. It's only fair. Is there someone who looks after your son during the day?'

'Mrs Millet,' Jenna offered.

'Then all it needs is for your husband to be at home in the evenings and at weekends, to give the boy a sense of security.'

'He can't.'

Her mind was jangling. How could she leave Christopher again? Ten days was far too long to dump him on Mrs Millet, and the prospect of asking her mother to take him again was daunting. Apart from which the heartbreak would crucify her.

'He must learn to be supportive.'

'What?' asked Jenna, not having returned from her problems.

'Your husband must help.'

'He won't—he can't,' she declared wildly. She clutched at Sam's hand, drawing strength from his calm, his comfort. 'Oh, Sam, what can I do?'

'There is one solution,' he said slowly. 'Take Christopher with you.'

# CHAPTER FIVE

STUPEFIED for a moment Jenna gazed at him, then relief washed all over her, running down her arms and legs, leaving her weak and laughing foolishly. 'What a great idea, why did I never think of that? Oh, Sam, you're wonderful!' She rested her head against his shoulder, rubbing her brow into the rounded muscle. 'Thank you, thank you!'

Her gratitude was making her incoherent and it was all she could do not to throw her arms around his neck and drown him in kisses. In the circumstances, taking Christopher along made sense, it was an obvious solution—and yet she knew it would never have occurred to her in a thousand years. Edward's conformity had rubbed off and she realised she had been conditioned to functioning between rigid guidelines. Work and family did not mix, and yet on this occasion, why not? Thank goodness Sam looked at life from a different angle.

'But what do I do with him when I interview Vivienne again?' she asked, her spirits plunging abruptly.

'Take him along. He doesn't bite, does he? Or kick the furniture? He's housetrained?'

'He's well behaved,' Jenna said indignantly, but thought it prudent to add, 'as a rule.'

'Well then . . .'

Happiness restored, she nuzzled against him like an exuberant pup, marvelling at him and his master stroke.

Sam's lips moved into a smile as he gazed down at her. 'Hey, it won't be roses all the way! The flight Down Under takes around twenty-four hours, it's quite an endurance test. Coping with a toddler could be one hell of a strain.'

'I'll manage.' She could manage anything with her son safely by her side.

'There'll be a visa to arrange and a ticket, but it's simple.'

'Just so long as no one at the office finds out.'

She pulled herself upright, suddenly aware she was cuddling up to him and enjoying the sensation!

'I'll keep quiet,' Sam smiled, releasing her hands in response to her unspoken request, for now he sensed she had drawn away from him on all levels.

'I know you will,' she began, then brought herself up short. *How* did she know he could be trusted? Wasn't he in the throes of writing an article which was in direct competition to her own? He was not the knight in shining armour she had imagined only seconds ago. How could he be? He was male, after all, and needed to be handled warily.

'Viv could pose a problem,' Sam mused. 'She has a tendency to blab. It's possible that in the future she might mention your son to Shelagh.'

'Couldn't you persuade her to be discreet?' For some reason Jenna fancied Sam's chances better than her own.

'I could try, but anyone who loves the sound of their own voice enough to talk for hours as she did earlier today has to be a risk. I'm sure she wouldn't deliberately shop you, but she does enjoy a gossip.'

Jenna recalled how Vivienne had blithely embarked on her revelations about Sam's background—though, to be fair, she had helped that particular conversation along herself.

'Perhaps I should come clean?' She was thinking aloud. 'Aren't the headquarters of the Desborough-Finch conglomerate located in Sydney?'

Sam was watching her closely. 'Yes, but so what?'

'If Mr Dèsborough-Finch was in residence I could go along to see him and explain all about Christopher. I'm sure he'd give me a fair hearing.'

'And thus you'd render Herbert Holt impotent if the fact that you're a mother ever became common knowledge?' He chuckled. 'My God, what a crafty young woman you are!'

'It's just an idea,' declared Jenna, disturbed to discover he was capable of adding two and two together, and making four.

'Just an idea! Don't pretend that computer brain of yours isn't flashing red lights! You'll pour yourself into your leather pants, swing into Kirby's office on those mile-long legs and have the poor bastard frothing at the mouth. Give him a glimpse of your gorgeous boobs and he'll probably sack Holt on the spot and make you editor of *The View* in his place! Why don't you wear . . .'

He added several *sotto voce* suggestions in the hope of making her blush. She did. Jenna hastily discovered that her fingernails held a lot of interest. How did you answer such flippancy? She had never met a man before who one minute treated her with such subtle thoughtfulness and the next with such careless insolence.

'I'm a serious political writer,' she protested, gathering her wits. 'My appearance has no bearing on the matter.'

He hooted with laughter. 'And why the hell do you imagine you're so successful? Okay,' he raised a hand to prohibit her interruption, 'I'm sure you write like a dream and have an excellent grasp of the political scenario, but if you're honest you must admit that the men you interview . . .' He broke off. 'I presume your politicians are chiefly men?' She nodded. 'Well, any redblooded male is either consciously, or subconsciously, going to respond to your appearance.' He raised his brows at the expression on her face. 'Sorry, honeybunch, but it's sex rearing its ugly head again.'

'It is *not*! I don't flirt, or wiggle my hips, or wear provocative clothes, or . . .'

'Jenna, Jenna, you have a lot to learn,' he sighed. 'Low cleavages and blatant come-hither looks are .a turn-off to many men, myself included, but the sight of a beautiful young woman striding around completely unaware of her own sexuality invites a response. And when you listen intently to all they have to say, wide eyes blue as subterranean pools, they're bound to fall hook, line and sinker. What man could ever resist such an attentive audience? I bet the politicians are far more garrulous with you than with some middle-aged male journalist.'

An announcement of their imminent arrival in London came over the intercom and Jenna considered his words.

'Perhaps there is some truth in what you say,' she conceded, adjusting her safety-belt.

She was not so blind as to be unaware that several of the politicians saved their juiciest titbits for her ears alone. She had established a good working relationship with members of the three major parties and now grudgingly accepted that there could be a slight bias towards her because she was young, blonde and female.

Sam helped her into her leather jacket.

'Why do you imagine Herbert Holt is so uptight about you?'

She had the answer off pat. 'Because he doesn't approve of female journalists, particularly female political journalists.'

Sam twisted, pushing his arms into his coat. 'You really are an innocent! One of the main reasons for his animosity is that you totally reject his appeal as a man.'

'*His* appeal!' Her mouth gaped open. 'He doesn't have any!'

'He imagines he does. Everyone has a streak of vanity in their make-up, even if they're pot-bellied and approaching sixty. Why do you think Herbert's such a snappy dresser? It's because he still rates his chances with the ladies. If you tried humouring him you'd probably discover his attitude towards you would soften.'

'Are you recommending I allow him to maul me?' she demanded.

'Hell, no! Is that what he would like?'

Jenna scowled. 'When I first started working at *The View* he used to come into my office on the pretext of seeing how I was progressing. He would stand close behind me and slide his hands over my shoulders. Ugh!' She shuddered.

'So you wouldn't touch him with a bargepole?'

'Never!'

The airline hostess was making her way along the aisle to check that tables had been stowed and seat-belts fastened. Jenna noticed that the smile the girl reserved for Sam was a hundred watts brighter than the one she bestowed on the grey-haired woman in front of him. Sexual attraction again, she presumed!

After returning the girl's smile, Sam continued the conversation. 'And I expect you've made damn sure Herbert is aware of your dislike?'

'I suppose so.'

'Use a bit of common sense,' he chided. 'No man likes to be rejected wholesale.' A shadow crossed his face. 'Not even me.' He rallied again. 'I know that you're married and I'm not suggesting anything ... illegal, but if you eased off the blatant dislike of Herbert it would be to your advantage.'

'I'll bear that in mind.' Jenna turned to look out of the porthole and when she saw the airport lights, she grinned. 'Back home.' She looked further. 'But no snow.'

Christopher was fast asleep, lying on his back, arms above his head, but she was unable to resist creeping into his room to kiss his petal-soft cheek. He stirred and she bent to tuck the quilt closer around him, whispering, 'Mummy's home,' in the vain hope that somehow he would absorb her presence and be comforted.

Mr and Mrs Millet rushed off to their own flat like homing pigeons.

'We didn't expect you back this evening, dearie, but now that you're here, we'll go,' Mrs Millet smiled.

'Stay the night,' Jenna protested, but they would have none of it.

'We'd rather be back in our own beds. When you get older you prefer to have your own things around you and settle back into the familiar routine. You understand?'

Yes, she did understand. She was far more at ease in her own home with Christopher sleeping soundly upstairs than in the Parisian hotel, comfortable though it had been. There was no place like home, Jenna decided. It was a cliché, but true, and she was lucky. Sam had merely exchanged one hotel for another.

'I'm going up to Scotland again,' he had said when they parted. 'I'll see you in the office towards the end of the week.' A thought struck him and he smiled. 'I hope the teddy-bear goes down well!'

At six o'clock the next morning Christopher awoke, crawling into Jenna's bed with great whoops of delight, kneeling on her stomach to smother her with fervent kisses, squeezing her neck and telling her that he had missed her and please would she not go away again?

'I won't, darling,' she promised, turning her head so that he wouldn't see the diamond-bright tears in her eyes. As a diversion she produced Sam's gift, and when her son had gleefully ripped away the paper he clutched the bear to him.

'Teddy-daddy,' he declared happily, running back to his bed to fetch his own smaller bear. 'This one teddy-boy,' he said, stabbing a plump finger into the threadbare tummy. 'And this one Teddy-daddy.' He rubbed the deliciously thick fur, smiling to himself, then cocked his head to one side and asked, 'Where's *my* daddy?'

'You don't have a daddy, Christopher,' she said, her voice choked. 'You just have a mummy who loves you very much.'

At that moment Jenna would gladly have thrown up her job and devoted her entire existence to him. But life was not so simple. She knew, at the back of her mind, she would be miserable without a career and a purpose in life. And if she was miserable, wouldn't that reflect on Christopher? Perhaps if she had more children she could find fulfilment at home, but her son already attended playgroup three mornings a week, and in a couple of years' time would be enrolled at proper school. What would she do with all her spare time then?

During the first eighteen months of his life she had lived in Manchester to comply with her parents' wishes, but had known the increasing creep of boredom due to a surfeit of coffee mornings and gossip. Try as she might, Jenna could raise no interest in discussion of duvets versus blankets, or what age toddlers should be dry at night. Her life with Edward, for all its drawbacks, had introduced her to a far wider range of interests. Staying at home was not for her.

By the time Christopher was heading for his second birthday she was practically climbing the walls. After weeks of heart-searching she came to a decision and asked her tenants to vacate the tiny London house. Of the two properties she now owned it had always been her favourite. The city house she considered 'hers',

whereas the larger Manchester home had borne the
stamp of her husband's personality. He had purchased
the suburban house several years before their marriage,
furnishing it in a comfortable conventional manner. In
many ways the Manchester house was superior to the
terraced dwelling, which had no garage and possessed
only a scrap of a garden.

'But it's a pied-à-terre!' her mother had shrieked
when Jenna revealed her intention of moving south.

'And quite big enough for Christopher and me,' she
retorted stubbornly, knowing she had a fight on her hands.

Over the next weeks her mother had cajoled and
pleaded, called upon Jenna's father to put his foot
down, ranted and raved over what she saw as a
catastrophic turn of events.

'I don't understand,' was her constant cry. 'Edward
intended that you sell the London house and stay in
Manchester permanently. Living alone in a big city
doesn't make sense!'

'It does to me.'

'But Edward . . .' her mother began.

'Edward is dead!' Jenna slammed, hearing her harsh
intonation and knowing she was shocking her mother
yet again.

'He planned it all!' the older woman screeched. 'Why
must you go against his wishes? Sometimes I think you
do it deliberately!'

How Jenna managed to sustain a note of reason she
did not know, but she did. 'I'm well aware you believe
Edward was incapable of making a faulty decision, but
when he planned what would happen after his death, he
didn't take my wishes into consideration.'

Her mother gasped, horrified at what she considered
akin to blasphemy. 'He did it all for you. When he
realised he had only a few months to live, he settled his
affairs in such a way that you would have no problems
when he was no longer around to protect you.'

Jenna flicked back her blonde curls from her shoulders. 'The plans he made were what *he* wished to happen, not what I wanted!'

'I don't understand you,' the cry came again, and she realised she was wasting her breath.

So the roomy house in the Manchester suburbs had been sold, together with much of the furniture. A few odd pieces she had had shipped down to London, but Edward's fringed and pleated lampshades, plummy velvet curtains and matching cushions, were at odds with the décor of the tiny terraced house. It had been purchased in the early days of their marriage—previously Edward had rented a bedsit—and Jenna had channelled all her artistic energies into its decoration and furnishing. Her enthusiasm had helped to deny the first glimmers that her future might not be the unmitigated bliss she had imagined. Natural wood, spring shades of lime and palest cinnamon, cool clean lines of plain walls hung with the occasional watercolour, shelves crammed with bright paperbacks; that was Jenna's style. Edward had been fondly patronising, saying that at her age she was allowed to have her head, but she had been delighted with the results then, and still loved the house nine years later.

Christopher trotted happily off to playgroup that morning with 'Teddy-daddy' clutched under his arm, and when Jenna returned to her desk at *The View* she was once more content, now brimming with smug anticipation at the prospect of Herbert's bombshell which he would be eager to drop. She did not have to wait long, for when he strutted into her office there was a gleam in his eye that indicated he was girded for battle, and she discovered that she wanted to smile.

After demanding a brief account of how she had fared in Paris he paused, searching for dramatic effect. 'Next week you'll fly to Australia to cover the premiere of the Valdis film in Sydney,' he announced, and folded his arms to await cries of anguish.

Jenna nodded meek acceptance. 'That's fine, thank you very much for this opportunity to travel.'

His mouth sagged. 'You don't mind?'

'No, I'm grateful for your generosity. First Paris, and now Australia!'

'But your mother?' he prompted faintly.

'She's fine.'

He leant forward, putting his palms flat on her desk. 'You'll be away ten whole days.'

'Marvellous! All that sunshine while you poor souls are shivering in sub-zero temperatures. It was snowing in Paris, so I expect it will be snowing here soon.'

Herbert scratched his head. 'You seem . . . different. Did something happen in Paris? You behaved yourself, didn't you?'

'What are you suggesting?' Jenna asked archly, smothering a grin.

'Nothing,' he muttered. 'But that young Australian bastard—well, he's—well . . .' Herbert adjusted his cravat. 'I know Shelagh finds him attractive.'

'I prefer Englishmen myself,' she said quickly.

'But mature ones?' he queried, obviously remembering Edward.

Jenna realised he was offering her a chance to realign their relationship which she would be foolish to miss.

'Yes, older men have much more to offer. They know how to treat a woman. Personally I find their refinement very appealing.' As she forced a coquettish smile, Jenna wondered if she was laying on the soft soap too thickly, but Herbert was too busy preening himself to notice any insincerity.

'Many women feel like that,' he told her. 'Intelligent women.' She could see him reassessing his opinion of her. He cleared his throat. 'Your outline for the Valdis article sounds excellent. I look forward to reading the final result when you return from Australia.'

To her surprise he produced a smile which was distinctly pleasant. There were a few more minutes of idle chatter, and then he wiggled his fingers in farewell and left. Oh, Sam, she thought, rocking with silent laughter, if only you could have seen this! But Sam was absent and, to her annoyance, she was only made aware of his return a few days later when Shelagh burst into her office and let it slip casually, on purpose, that she had spent the previous evening in the Australian's company.

'I didn't know he was back from Scotland,' said Jenna, making a great show of tidying her papers.

Why should she feel so irritated? Shelagh was an attractive girl, unattached and agreeable, and Sam was a young man alone in London—what was more natural than that they should join forces? Nevertheless the idea dismayed her. Good grief, I can't be jealous, she thought. Sam was a friend, that much she accepted but, unlike Shelagh, she had no intention of becoming further involved with him.

The girl perched on the corner of the desk, swinging a shapely ankle. 'Sam hasn't been into the office on purpose. He has some project on the go and he's been working on it at his hotel.'

Jenna's mouth thinned. Some project! He was writing his article and keeping it under wraps.

'I expect you spent a lot of time discussing Vivienne Valdis?' she said. It was one of those flat statements with a question mark attached. Sam would be filling in any blank spaces by coaxing Shelagh to give him her impressions of the actress.

'She was mentioned, so were other things! He's a great guy, isn't he? I wish I'd had the chance of going to gay Paree with him.'

'The trip was very interesting,' Jenna allowed stiffly.

The other girl giggled. 'So nothing happened?'

Her cheeks grew pink. 'Of course not!'

'Why of course? Sam and I are going out again this

evening, and if nothing happens I shall be very disappointed.' Shelagh swung towards the door, pausing to lean against it body arched provocatively, one hand at her hip. 'If you loosened up, Jenna, you'd discover what a fantastic place the world can be.'

When Christopher was tucked up in bed that evening and the house was silent, Jenna found her thoughts returning to Shelagh's words. Since she had moved down to London life had been challenging, full of career interest but, she admitted, hardly *fantastic*! At least, not Shelagh's idea of fantastic. She and Christopher shared many good times, but he was only a little boy and his conversation and needs were simple. His latest pleasure was in tickling her. When she pretended to squirm in response to his poky fingers, he would giggle uncontrollably, rocking with delight at himself and her. But was a tickling session with her small son to be the highlight of her life? Didn't she have other needs? Once she would have said categorically *no*, but now she wondered . . .

Jenna picked up a magazine which Mrs Millet had left behind and thumbed restlessly through the pages. Why, all of a sudden, did the future for which she had fought with such determination loom like an abyss before her? Was she destined to spend the rest of her life sitting alone at night with only the moan of the wintry wind for company? She stared down at a fashion spread, the models luminous in outfits of sequined mauve and pink satin—'Dresses for Your Disco Dates' the headline screamed. Disco dates, she thought disconsolately—when was she ever likely to go to a disco? True, she had had the chance in Paris, but she would have been a fish out of water.

She turned the page. Here was a before-and-after article in which a middle-aged woman had been snatched from the street and transformed into a raving beauty; all by having her hair styled, eyebrows shaped and face made up by a well-known cosmetics firm. Jenna read the details. 'A good night cream is essential for the over-thirties,' the copy ran. 'Watch out for those tiny giveaway lines around the eyes.' 'To keep a youthful supple outline you must exercise regularly.' Jenna flung the magazine aside in disgust. Here she was, on the brink of middle age and destined to turn fat and flabby, wrinkled like a prune. The days for having fun had disappeared before she had had any! When I get to Sydney I'll go to the Wild Cockatoo, she decided, I'll dance and swing my hips and I'll flirt and . . . She stopped short. But the night at the disco did not include her, did it? Sam and Vivienne were both carefree and unfettered, but she had Christopher.

Her thoughts jarred. She was being greedy. It was impossible to have everything. Her decision to become pregnant, despite Edward's opposition, had been deliberate, though their infrequent lovemaking had meant she had virtually given up hope before the doctor at last confirmed she was to have a baby. By that time Edward had been too wound up in his illness and his obsession for tidying up the remnants of his life to care much either way. Jenna shivered, realising, to her surprise, that the fire had burned low. She threw on more logs and when they were crackling, the orange flames leaping high in the hearth, she abandoned her introspection and instead considered her list.

A variety of chores had to be completed before the flight to Australia in two days' time. Christopher's ticket and visa had been easily obtained, now she must attend to his clothes. How he had grown over the past few months! She had whipped him in and out of his summer shorts and tee-shirts, discarding those which were too tight. It was doubtful the few remaining sets would be sufficient for ten days, but she could always buy extra items in Sydney. Tomorrow she would cancel the papers, stop the milk, ask Mrs Millet if she would be kind enough to call in every other day to remove the mail from behind the front door, and she would take her car into the garage and have it repaired while she was abroad.

The carriage-clock on the bookshelves showed nine. Time was dragging its heels, and in an attempt to push it along Jenna decided to take a bath. After a long soak she dried herself, lavishly sprinkling on a flowery talcum powder. What a waste, she thought ruefully, stroking the fine powder along her arms and legs, here I am smelling delicious and nobody knows, or cares! She wrinkled her nose at her pale-blue winceyette pyjamas. It was as well she was alone, for the pyjamas were unimpressive. Bought with one requirement in mind—warmth—they covered her up par excellence, long sleeves and trousers snugly ribbed at wrist and ankle. She found herself wondering how Sam and Shelagh were getting along. Shelagh wouldn't be seen dead in thick-knit pyjamas. No doubt she paraded around in rustling black satin, slits up to her thighs and a plunging neckline.

Defiantly knotting the sash of her towelling robe, Jenna stomped downstairs. What was wrong with her this evening? She subsided on to the sofa, sighing because the stupid fingers on the stupid clock still hadn't managed to reach ten. Her restlessness must be Sam's fault. His assertion of life's sensualities had reopened an awareness of her own faults in that direction. Prior to meeting him, she had been content with her independent lifestyle, but now she was unhappily aware that sections could be sterile. He had prompted her to delve into her own psyche, and what she had discovered was disturbing. On the edge of deeper thought, Jenna halted. Why resurrect painful memories? The time for heart-searching, for frustration and the inevitable retreat, were over. An emotional harbour had been reached where she was safe from the buffeting waves of love and passion and desire, and there she fully intended to stay.

The doorbell chimed, breaking into her thoughts. Not the milkman *now*! He had a habit of calling round at odd times and until recently she had believed he came because he liked to talk to Christopher, but now she began to wonder ... Before she opened the door she took the precaution of slipping the chain into position. He was a friendly type, but she was damned if she would allow him into her house at this time of night. She wrenched open the door.

'Sam!' Her pulse accelerated in alarm. 'What do you want?'

He was positioned on the step like a monolith, his hair shadowy beneath the conflicting light of street lamps and moon, his shoulders massive beneath the sheepskin coat.

'I want an explanation,' he growled.

'An explanation?'

When he shifted, she saw he was angry, for the strong jaw was bitten down tight and his brown eyes glittered with fevered rage. In apprehension her fingers curled around the latch.

'Open up ... please.' His low voice held a dash of menace.

Just for a moment Jenna wondered if she dared refuse. Surely it was wiser to keep him at bay? But there was too much aggression in his tone, in his stance, and she recognised that in this mood the muscled Australian was quite capable of slamming a shoulder and forcing an entry. Doing as she was told, she opened up, and he strode impatiently into the narrow hall.

'May I take your coat?' she asked, acting the gracious hostess partly by instinct, partly to allow her galloping nerves a chance to steady.

She knew exactly what explanation he was demand-

ing. Sam had unearthed her lies and was now aware
that her husband was dead and she had been a widow
for a number of years. All along it had been inevitable
that he must discover the truth, but, like so much else,
she had whisked the thought aside, preferring not to
face up to what would happen next. A hasty look at his
dark expression showed her the time had come for her
to pay for her deceit.

'I want to see Christopher,' he snapped, tugging
fractiously at the cuffs of his oatmeal-coloured sweater.
Hanging up his coat, Jenna swivelled in surprise, her
blue eyes wide. This wasn't the attack she had expected.
'Let's see if *he* exists,' Sam sneered.

'He does!'

He placed icy fingers on her shoulder, pushing her
towards the staircase. 'Show me.'

She mounted the stairs, sensitive to his heavy tread
behind her. When they reached the landing, she paused.
'He's asleep,' she whispered.

'I don't intend to disturb him,' came the curt reply.

Together they went into the small bedroom where the
subdued light from the landing showed her son curled
up among the rumpled blankets, snug in his sleepsuit.
In the stillness they could hear the steady rise and fall of
his breathing. Sam looked down at the little boy, at the
silver-blond curls shining in the half-light, at the long
lashes fanning the smooth cheeks, and said nothing. He
waited as Jenna bent to tuck the covers over the
sleeping child and followed her in silence down the
stairs. When she led him into the living-room, he stood
with his back to the fire, warming himself.

Jenna perched on the arm of the sofa, too much on
edge to relax. 'Well?' she demanded, knowing the only
way to maintain any credibility was to meet attack with
attack.

'Now I want to see your husband,' he growled.

She laced her fingers together and hooked them

around her knee. 'You know I don't have one.' Her
fingers were tense, whitening as the blood drained.

'How very kind of you to tell me,' he jeered, then
paused and added contemptuously, 'at last!'

She was committed to defending her action. 'I
thought it was preferable to say I was married.'

'Why?' The air vibrated with emotion and the space
between them yawned wide. 'Did you imagine if I knew
you were a widow, I would pounce?' Sam demanded.

'Well, no,' she said, trying for blasé indifference, not
blushing confusion. Confusion won. 'It ... it just
seemed like a good idea at the time.'

Sam stuck his thumbs into his waistband, drumming
his fingers on the hard plane of his stomach. 'Shelagh
tells me you freeze off all the men at work.'

'If I do it's because I don't want anyone to find out
about Christopher,' she flashed.

'Nonsense!'

She ignored his retort, her hand flying to her throat
in panic. 'You didn't tell Shelagh I had a child?'

He shook his head wearily. 'Why do you insist on
building a fortress, Jenna? Hell, you fling down boiling
oil on anyone who even approaches in friendship. What
are you afraid of?'

Her spine grew rigid. 'I'm not afraid of anything.'

'Then why fight so hard to keep everyone at arm's
length? And don't dare to say because of Christopher,'
he warned. He subjected her to a steady discerning look
which made her want to look away. 'Shelagh tells me
your husband died three years ago. Have you had any
lovers since?'

'Lovers? You mean boy-friends?'

A shadow flickered across Sam's face. 'I damn well
mean *lovers*! Men who have climbed naked into your
bed and made love to you.'

She stared at him aghast, the imagery behind her eyes
too great. 'You don't have to be so ... so brash!'

'Yes, I do, honeybunch, as long as you insist on denying reality. The only way to get through to you is to call a spade a bloody shovel!' He reached down to grip her shoulders, pulling her up to stand before him. 'You're a beautiful, desirable woman, Jenna. You're made to be cherished, you're made for love.' His fingers tightened as she made to pull away. 'You *are*! he insisted huskily.

'I'm not!'

There was a quick smile as he bent his head to brush his mouth across her lips.

'No!' She thrashed ineffectually in his arms.

'Yes, my darling, oh yes!'

Her lips quivered beneath his. He was playing havoc with her senses, but how could she cope? His mouth was warm and firm, and as he coaxed her lips apart the male moistness of his kiss lit a burst of multi-coloured rockets that exploded in her head, one by one. Edward had never had this effect. The hard demanding surge of Sam's body against hers aroused a feeling she had never known before and she found herself clinging to him. The kiss deepened. Oh God! he was eating her alive, and as it went on it became mutual. She was enraptured by the taste of him, the bruising eagerness of his mouth. There were more kisses and more until Jenna knew Sam was turning her to liquid. Somehow Sam had loosened the sash of her robe and pushed aside her pyjama top to rub his hand into the pit of her back, pressing her deeper against him. He rested his face against the golden mist of her hair.

'You smell of roses,' he murmured.

His lips grazed her brow and her skin tingled, alive with an exquisite awareness of him. He kissed her again, slowly, deeply, nibbling at the edges of her mouth and drawing a response which had Jenna's heart spinning giddily.

'I think I'm falling in love with you,' he whispered, smiling into her eyes.

'You can't—you mustn't!' she squeaked, pushing from him as far as she could, which wasn't far because Sam's hold was firm, his fingers splayed across the nakedness of her back.

'Why can't I? Why mustn't I?' he demanded throatily, catching her earlobe between his teeth and sucking with seductive gentleness.

How could she line up an argument when he was so close, so absorbed in pleasuring her? He was stroking her spine, his hands sliding over the silken fragrant skin in a manner which had an alarming effect on her equilibrium.

'We hardly know each other,' she said in a precarious tremolo. The words sounded trite, even to her.

'I have enough experience to realise we'd be good for one another,' murmured Sam, his brown eyes wandering lazily across her face to stop on the tempting fullness of her slightly parted lips.

'We wouldn't be! It's too soon! We come from different countries,' she babbled wildly, and felt his lips crease into a smile as he dipped his head further to kiss her throat.

'What do you imagine love is, honeybunch, something neat and orderly, like painting by numbers? You don't have to start in the top left-hand corner and work in rotation using X colour for X shape, keeping within the lines. Emotions aren't so predictable. Love bursts upon you like a sudden slash of colour, and that's that.'

He pushed her pyjama top further and slid his hands to feel the sideways swell of her naked breasts flattened against his chest, deliberately allowing himself no further caress for the time being. Sam knew she could not be rushed. Despite her years of marriage she was tentative about lovemaking, he could feel the reserve within her. There were barriers to surmount before she would be ready to accept the adoration he longed to lay at her feet.

'I don't think I've ever been in love,' she said into his neck, her lips brushing his ear.

Sam held himself very still, aware of the satiny grace of her body, wanting her so much that he had to grit his teeth, forcing himself to keep calm. A moment of intensity tore at him and when he cupped her breasts she felt the shiver of her tautening nipples, a low moan escaped from his throat.

'Jenna—oh God, *Jenna!*' All his longing was wrapped up in the way he spoke her name.

A log fell noisily in the grate and he used the diversion to haul his hands back down to her waist. He would not have been surprised if beads of perspiration were standing out on his brow, but when he wiped the skin it was dry.

'Would you like a cup of coffee?' Jenna asked, sensing his withdrawal and not knowing whether to feel disappointed or consoled. A wisp of nervous laughter escaped, relieving her tension, and she stepped from him, refastening the belt of her robe.

Taking a deep breath, Sam rubbed his knuckles across his jaw. 'No,' then he thought to add, 'thank you.' He studied her gravely. 'Jenna, we should talk.'

'Did you have a good dinner with Shelagh?' she asked simultaneously, and they both laughed.

The fragility of the moment shattered, and now they were on an easier footing.

'I'm afraid I wined and dined Shelagh with undue haste and rushed her straight back home. As you can imagine, she wasn't too thrilled,' he grinned, having chosen to follow the easier of the two threads of conversation. 'We'd barely met when she made some chance reference to your husband's death, and from then on all I could think about was coming round here and confronting you.' He sank down on to the sofa, pulling her on to his knee. Okay, so he wasn't going to make love to her tonight, but he still wanted to touch her. 'Relax,' he smiled. 'You're safe!'

Jenna allowed herself to lie back against his shoulder.
'I'm sorry I lied, Sam.'

She looked at his hand which lay across her thigh
because it was too hard to look up into his face. He had
large hands, long tanned fingers with the nails cut
straight across, a smattering of golden hairs on the
knuckles.

'What did Shelagh say about Edward?' she asked
cautiously.

If Maggi had cut through her husband's veneer of
urbane charm, might not others be as acute? His widow
would be the last to hear any rumours which might
have circulated, and perhaps Edward had had a
reputation for being a cold fish. What gossip was there
behind her back? Suddenly it was difficult to breathe.

'Only that he died of cancer.' Sam's thumb began to
move back and forth on the towelling robe covering her
thigh. 'I imagine he never saw Christopher?'

'No. I was only a few months pregnant when he died.'

'It's a shame that your husband missed knowing he
had a son.'

'Edward didn't want children.' Her voice shifted
gears into a false brightness. 'He hated any upheaval,
any mess. I dare say Christopher would have been
banished to a nursery if Edward had lived.' She glanced
at the spillage from the toybox in the corner, the
spinning top lying on the bookcase. 'Everything in his
domain had to be neat and tidy, and he expected
everyone to conform. He was a despot, a kind despot,
but a despot all the same. To be blunt . . .' Jenna
paused. Should she admit this? She had never revealed
the sentiment to anyone before. There was a *soupçon* of
guilt. She swallowed hard.

Sam waited, his dark eyes impassive. Whatever Jenna
had to say, she must say it without any prompting from
him. He heard the rasp of her breathing, could feel the
tension stringing her nerves.

'To be blunt, it was a relief when he died. He ruled me for six years,' she said bitterly, and closed her eyes. 'But I'll never be ruled again.' The blue eyes snapped open and she swept from his knee to stand glaring fiercely down, fists clenched in the pockets of her robe. In some curious way her anger was channelled at Sam. 'I answer to no one now, and that's the way it's going to stay.'

She was warning him, he knew, and the knowledge flooded him with resentment. Why should he be punished for her husband's faults? He slid a hand beneath his jersey to rub his midriff.

'Okay, lady, keep on fighting,' he drawled, lounging back in the corner of the sofa, his long legs stretched out before him.

The mood had changed. Gone was the demure kitten who had accepted his caresses, trembling as his hands had wandered over her, making little purrs of pleasure. Now she was a tiger, a she-cat determined to conquer the world on behalf of herself and her cub, on *her* terms. Sam knew she had emotional problems, problems she would have to work through all by herself, problems which, for the time being, she was not prepared to share.

'I must go,' he said abruptly, rising to his feet. 'I don't want to give your neighbours cause to gossip. You have your reputation to protect.' The remark contained more bite than humour.

Jenna read the fingers on the carriage-clock. 'It's past midnight!'

'How time flies when you're having fun.'

The words were droll, but she shot him a look of deep suspicion. Was that a joke or wasn't it? Sam was unperturbed, and as she followed him out into the narrow hall, her anger fizzled away.

'I'm looking forward to visiting Australia,' she said brightly.

'Are you organised with Christopher's visa and ticket?' he asked, dragging on his heavy coat.

'Yes, as you said, it was straightforward.' She smiled. 'And he loves the teddy-bear.'

'Good.' He was fastening the buttons, working down his jacket, and she found herself mesmerised by the movements of his fingers. 'I'll see you at the airport.'

Her brow puckered. 'You're not coming into the office?'

'I've decided to spend most of tomorrow . . .' he checked his watch and changed it to, 'most of today, with Vivienne. We're having a photo session at her place.'

Jenna adopted a phony nonchalance. 'That'll be nice. I went round to see her earlier this week, just for a morning. She's continuing the honesty line.'

'Be careful,' he warned. 'All may not be what it seems, she could still change her mind.'

Jenna flicked back her hair. It seemed that *Sam* had changed his mind. Only minutes before he had hinted he was falling in love with her, but in a few hours' time he would be cavorting with Vivienne. His talk of love must have been double-talk, a standard bachelor's ploy—doubtless the required lead-up to intimacy, she decided with scorn.

Her heart missed a beat. *Sam* had drawn back from their lovemaking, not she. She had been on fire, too aroused to think straight, let alone control what happened between them. Her face clouded. But later she had made it brutally clear love was not for her, that she had no intention of allowing a man to get up close again. If, as a result, his interest had switched to Vivienne she could not blame him. The actress would doubtless entertain Sam as he wished to be entertained. Jenna knew she should be grateful he had chosen to spend his time elsewhere, but instead she was stinging with annoyance. She gave herself a private talking-to.

Why not accept that Sam was an easy-living, easy-loving, easy-talking bachelor who ran his life to suit himself, not her! She must not fall into the trap of trusting him. The facts spoke volumes. This evening he had dated Shelagh, then visited her, and tomorrow he would be charming Vivienne. Another thought hit her—no doubt he would be using the so-called photo session to squeeze out fresh material for *his* article. God, he was underhanded! She pulled wide the door with an unnecessary show of ill-tempered force, making the corner of Sam's mouth twist. He was amused, very likely at her. Well, he could go and take a running jump . . .

'You don't approve of my connection with Viv, do you?' he asked, turning up his collar as he viewed the cold night air.

'She's very nice,' Jenna replied stiffly, realising he was well on the way to reading her mind again. She *did* like Vivienne, now that she had discarded the film-star image and the dreadful Josh, but she resented Sam spending tomorrow with her. She knew she shouldn't, but she did!

His grin dived into a husky chuckle. 'Nice! That's the kiss of death if I ever heard one! And speaking of kisses, I'll have one.' His brown eyes sparkled. 'If you have one to spare.'

Her chin jutted high. 'I don't. I thought I'd made it abundantly clear that I'd like us to be . . . just friends.'

He stood in front of her, pushing the door closed until she heard it click.

'No, honeybunch, you didn't do that,' he murmured softly. 'It's no use your head saying "no" to me when your body says "yes" so very definitely.' He reached out to pull her into his arms, ignoring the way she was holding herself to attention.

'Sam I don't . . .' she protested.

'Jenna, you *do*! he mocked, and then his mouth covered hers.

The touch of his lips was electric, sending shockwaves pulsing down her arms and legs until her toes curled. Her lips parted and her arms slid around his neck, her fingers burrowing into the thick hair at the nape. Her instant arousal dismayed her, and yet it was, she realised, only the tip of the iceberg. But she could think no further, because his hands were sliding beneath her pyjama top to her ribcage, his fingertips brushing the underswell of her breasts. He was so strong, so sure as he rolled the silken peaks between thumb and forefinger until she found herself buckling against him, a low animal sound straining from deep within her. There was a quiver of rapture like a flame and she fell against him, half-sobbing into his neck.

'Darling, darling,' he soothed, stroking her hair. He replaced her pyjama top and held her, rocking her in his arms like a father comforting a distressed child.

'Go, Sam,' she implored when she was capable of speech. 'Please go!' The pitch of her emotions terrified her. Why did she react so wildly to his caresses? So much, so soon?

'Don't be frightened, my darling. This is what love is all about,' he said tenderly.

She raised stricken eyes to his. 'I've never felt like this before.'

He smiled. 'But you will again, I promise you.'

# CHAPTER SIX

LOVE must be an infectious disease, given the right conditions, Jenna decided, pumping fractiously at her pillow for what seemed to be the twentieth time. After Sam's departure she had gone to bed and had proceeded to toss and turn for half the night. Her brain had swung, circled, veered off at tangents great and small, but invariably had returned to Sam and the dangerous effect he was wreaking on her emotions. He had spoken of love, and now she found her thoughts drifting off along similar lines, which was impossible.

Before his arrival that evening she had been lonely and a trifle despondent. His large male presence had had a curiously comforting quality which must have accounted for her rash response to his kisses. Jenna lay on her back, eyes open wide in the darkness. But Sam was intrinsic dynamite. He was capable of blasting a gaping hole in her defences if she gave him half the chance. The trouble was that she *liked* him. His mention of them having met in a previous life didn't seem too far-fetched. Indeed, when she had first set eyes on him at the newspaper offices, it had been as though an invisible lasso had encircled them, and now it was tightening, drawing them closer and closer.

Twisting to lie on her stomach, she dragged the bedclothes around her ears. But she had no wish for intimacy—especially a relationship with some fine desperado from the other side of the world, a relationship which was bound to end in disaster. Well, it would if Sam ever managed to get her into bed. His kisses she enjoyed, this evening had proved that, but anything further . . .

124

There was little point in crossing bridges in advance. A dose of Christopher would cool Sam's ardour. He had seen her son at his least destructive—fast asleep like a curly-mopped cherub—but once he had had a dose of him awake Sam would realise the implications of becoming involved with a young woman *plus* small child. Two-year-olds stuck their fingers into your ears, wet their pants, threw tantrums, broke ornaments and then left you high and dry in your rage by flinging chubby arms around your neck to deposit sticky kisses. Yes, even if her own resistance to Sam was precarious, she could rely on her son to send him on his way.

The departure hall was thronged. Many long-haul jets left for their destinations in the evening, and seven o'clock seemed to be a peak period. With a determined grip on Christopher's hand, Jenna pushed her way through the solid mass of travellers, tucking herself in at the end of the queue for the Australian flight. She set down her suitcase and released her son. 'Teddy-daddy' was clasped to his chest and now that his thumb was available he stuck it into his mouth and sucked noisily. She knew he was tired; he would probably sleep once they were on the plane. But at present the little boy was wide-eyed, missing nothing of the scurry of passengers to left and right, the colourful mix of different nationalities, the greetings and farewells.

'Look, funny man!' he laughed, pointing a finger at a man in a red fez.

Jenna hoped the man had not overheard or, if he had, that he did not understand. She inspected her watch. They were early, but early on purpose. She intended to check in and reserve seats for herself and Christopher before Sam arrived. It was unfair to lumber him with the two of them. If he sat beside her he would feel duty bound to help with her son, and she felt there was no reason why he should be thrust into that situation. In any case, she could manage perfectly well on her own.

When the queue moved Jenna pushed her suitcase forward with her knee. Because the weather was still icy, she was wearing her leather trousers and flying-jacket, and had dressed Christopher in a crimson anorak and dungarees, a knitted woollen bobble-hat covering his silver-white curls. The first stop was Bahrein, and there she intended to discard a few layers for the pair of them. The Bahrein climate was hot, so the Sports Editor had informed her; even though they were landing in the middle of the night it might well be ninety degrees. Seven hours after Bahrein came Singapore which was almost on the Equator, and another seven hours flying later, Sydney.

'How's my long-legged beauty?' a voice with an Australian twang asked, and a cold beaky nose nuzzled deep into her hair. Sam spun her round and kissed her soundly, then stood back, grinning at her flustered confusion.

'You kissed my mummy!' accused Christopher in a loud clear voice, and people in the queue turned to smile.

Jenna's cheeks burned and to cover the helter-skelter race of her heart she bent to her son and picked him up.

'This is Mr Wood,' she explained. 'He bought you your new teddy, so what do you say?'

'Thank you.' It was a whisper, for the little boy was overcome with shyness in the light of Sam's smile and buried his face into Jenna's shoulder.

'And what's your name?' Sam asked, tugging gently at a silver tendril which had escaped from the crimson hat.

Christopher raised his head, plump bottom lip pouting as he subjected the stranger to a wary inspection. 'Christopher,' he offered grudgingly.

Sam prodded the teddy-bear clutched to the little boy's chest. 'And who's this?'

'Teddy-daddy.'

The queue shuffled forward, and Jenna repeated her trick with her knee and suitcase. 'You don't have to sit with us,' she offered hastily. 'I quite understand if you prefer to sit on your own and get some sleep.'

'Do I look so worn out?' Sam enquired, tilting his head.

'No.'

Indeed his appearance was that of a man mentally and physically alert, his sultry tan and two-tone hair accentuating the vibrant sun-god image. She wondered how he would look with bathing trunks in place of the sheepskin jacket and blue jeans, but rejected the vagrant thought. Just one more couple to go and then they would reach the head of the queue.

'Stand down, Christopher,' she said, bending. 'I have to find our tickets.'

The glistening thumb came from his mouth. 'Don't want to.'

'Just for a moment,' she began, feeling him resist.

'I'll take him.' Sam whisked the little boy into his arms. There was a borderline decision to be made; Christopher didn't know whether to laugh or cry. His lower lip trembled, then Sam gave him a wide wink and that clinched matters. Christopher giggled.

'Mr Wood will look after you,' said Jenna, searching in her duffle-bag for the folder containing passport and tickets.

'Mr Wood's rather formal, call me Sam.'

Christopher looked into his face with innocent blue eyes.

'Daddy Sam,' he declared.

Jenna's cheeks grew pink once more. 'Just Sam,' she insisted, but from the corner of her eye she could see amusement tugging at Sam's mouth.

Her son's lower lip jutted. '*Daddy* Sam!'

She raised her eyes to the ceiling and sighed. 'I'm

sorry. He's going through a stage of tagging "Daddy" on to every man he meets. He does it with Mr Millet and the milkman,' she added, gathering steam. 'And they're both grandfathers!' Somehow she was desperate to make it plain that the 'Daddy' meant nothing, nothing at all.

'What's that?' asked Christopher, jamming a stubby finger against Sam's teeth.

'A gap.' Sam lifted a finger towards the little boy's front teeth. 'Like yours.'

Christopher had spaces between his teeth like many small children, and Jenna was about to embark on an explanation when the airline official held out his hand for their tickets.

'All together?' he nodded at the three of them, but he had taken it for granted.

'All together,' Sam confirmed.

Their luggage was docketed, boarding passes handed over, and Sam led the way towards the escalator, Christopher still in his arms. Jenna followed behind.

'Are you returning to the U.K. when this assignment is over, or staying in Australia?' she asked sharply. If she was able to set a limit on their time together she would feel happier, better able to control events with the knowledge that Sam's presence was merely an interlude.

He hoisted Christopher further up into his arms. 'I'm coming back here. I start shooting in Scotland in four weeks' time.'

She stepped on to the moving staircase behind him. 'Shooting deer?' she exlaimed in amazement, looking up.

'Yes, among other things.'

They reached the upper level.

'Do you derive pleasure from killing animals?' she asked, showing her displeasure.

Sam burst out laughing. 'I'm not killing them, I'm making a documentary on wildlife for a television series in Australia.'

Jenna's mind pitched and tossed. 'But I ... I didn't know you made films,' she protested weakly.

When they reached the departure lounge Sam sat down on one of the long benches and hoisted Christopher up on to his knee. 'You don't know much about me at all, honeybunch, do you? And that's because you never ask.' His brown eyes trapped hers and she had no willpower to look away. 'And the reason you don't ask is because you're scared stiff that I might move in too close. As long as you can persuade yourself I'm a mere acquaintance, then you're safe. But allow me to get under your skin, which is what I fully intend to do,' he gave her a look of impish warmth, 'then how do you resist me?'

'If you imagine I find you irresistible, you're extremely arrogant,' she retorted, taking umbrage.

He howled softly. 'Jenna, you can't let me make love to you one evening and two days later pretend I'm a business colleague and nothing more!'

'We *didn't* make love,' she hissed in an undertone, giving a quick look at Christopher, but he had slumped against Sam's chest, sucking his thumb, and appeared to be half asleep. 'That was just ... a few kisses.'

Sam laced his fingers with hers, tightening his grip to prevent her pulling away. 'That was *foreplay*!' Startled, her blue eyes shot open wide, making Sam chuckle. 'I'm sorry if the word shocks you, but that's what it was—and very stimulating, too!'

Jenna glared at him. 'Must you be so ... so ...'

'Brash, I believe you called me.'

'You are, you're brash and arrogant and ...' She was lost for words.

'And I'm a warm, meaningful human being,' he teased. 'Once you get to know me.'

'I don't intend to!'

His eyes danced gleefully. 'You didn't intend to indulge in foreplay, but you did, *and* it set you on fire.'

Jenna had an ominous feeling that Sam, alone, was controlling their conversation, but she refused to fall apart.

'And have you made any other wildlife documentaries?' she demanded.

'She said as she scuttled back behind the ramparts,' Sam mocked.

She stuck out her tongue in a rash display of fury, but he only leant forward and kissed her full on the mouth, which left her more bemused than ever.

'Yes, I have.' Ripples of amusement were rocking his chest, and suddenly Christopher sat upright.

'Where's the plane?' he asked.

'Outside,' said Sam. 'Shall we go and take a look?'

They disappeared along the corridor and Jenna slumped back, totally drained. Sam's outspoken attitude had been bad enough to cope with before, when he had believed her to be married, but now! Now it was ten times worse. She was convinced he came out with outrageous statements on purpose, and the trouble was she invariably rose to the bait. She really must aim for a cooler reaction in future. What a contrast Sam made to Edward! She could not recall her husband cracking a single sexual joke throughout the entire length of their marriage, in fact he rarely cracked *any* jokes; he had been far too earnest for that. Edward had believed every moment of the day should be usefully employed, and had worked hard and long on behalf of his constituents. Too hard and too long, for there had been little left over for his private life and for her . . .

Christopher did not sleep on the first leg of the flight. After seeing the plane he perked up, and when they boarded there was enough happening to keep him bright-eyed and bushy-tailed, though it was long past his bedtime. He tucked into dinner with gusto, beaming when the steward patted his head, saying how well behaved he was. Later he discovered another little boy in the seat ahead, and the two of them had a great game of peep-bo until their squeals of delight threatened to disrupt the peace and Jenna called a halt. After that he calmed down and sat on Sam's knee to listen to a tale about Australia.

'Once upon a time there was a baby kangaroo who lived in Warrumbungle,' began Sam, and the little boy ahead poked through the gap between the seats to listen.

'Bungle?' repeated Christopher, giggling fit to bust.

'One day this kangaroo's mummy made him a great big Pavlova.'

'What's Pavlova?' asked the little boy ahead, who looked to be around five years old.

'A pudding made from meringue and fruit and cream.' Sam patted Christopher's tummy. 'You can have some when we arrive in Sydney.'

'Can I have some, too?' asked the other little boy.

'You'd better have a word with your daddy.'

Christopher slapped a none-too-gentle hand against Sam's jaw. 'You Daddy Sam, *my* daddy.'

'No, he's not,' Jenna chided sleepily.

Everything was deliciously hazy for the glasses of Australian wine Sam had coaxed her to drink with dinner had had a soporific effect. No longer did the image of him as Christopher's father strike alarm in her heart. The idea now had a fascination, for he was the right age, the right colouring, and was showing the correct degree of amused interest to fill the role.

'Why don't you rest up, honeybunch?' Sam asked, tucking the blanket around her shoulders. 'I'll look after the Boy Wonder.'

'Are you sure?' she murmured, but her lids were closing and within moments she had drifted into oblivion.

Jenna awoke when the plane was descending into Bahrein.

'Oh, heavens—I'm sorry,' she apologised when she discovered to her horror she had been asleep for nearly three hours. She frowned at her son who was looking at pictures as Sam pointed them out in the airline magazine. 'Did he sleep?'

'Not a wink, he's been chattering non-stop. We even had a sample of the tickling I understand you enjoy.'

'Has he been to the loo?' she asked cautiously, fearing the worst.

'Four times. It's a good job we're in the aisle seat.'

'I'm sorry,' she gasped, starting up with the apologies again.

Sam laughed. 'Don't worry, I have a tribe of nephews, so I'm quite capable of dealing with the requirements of little boys.'

'Thanks a lot.' Jenna couldn't resist squeezing his wrist.

The airport terminal at Bahrein was air-conditioned, so the temperature change was not as violent as she had feared, though it was still warm enough to set aside their jackets. After a stop-over of barely an hour while the plane refuelled, they boarded again.

'This time I'll entertain Christopher and you rest,' Jenna told Sam, but as soon as the plane swept up into the sky and levelled off her son fell fast asleep. She settled him down on his seat with the blanket tucked around him.

'Now you go to sleep,' she commanded Sam again, but he grinned.

'I need a thumb to suck and mine's too big. I want yours.'

This time she was ready for him. 'Okay,' she agreed, but first she checked that no one else could see. 'Here you are.'

He gave a low sexy growl and made a bite at the thumb she held towards him. The sucking had a disturbing effect and Sam knew what he was doing all right, she could read it in the shrewd gleam of his eyes. There was the pressure of his teeth and his tongue against her skin, a warm wet suction which was curiously erotic.

'It feels nice,' she said in surprise.

He removed her thumb, but caught at her hand so that it did not stray too far from his mouth. 'Naturally it's nice, why do you think kids do it?'

Jenna shrugged. Sam took another swift pull, bending his head to hers as she began to laugh.

'Flavour of the month,' he grinned. 'Sweet blonde journalist, a dreamy concoction but with some tart slivers.'

A stewardess appeared along the aisle and Jenna pulled away her thumb. The film was due to start and cabin lights were being doused. When they both decided they were not interested in watching the show, Jenna tried to persuade Sam he should sleep.

'Honestly, I'm not tired,' he said. 'Besides, I only want to sleep with you.' He stopped the stewardess as she passed. 'Please would you bring us some more of that white wine?'

'Certainly, sir.'

The wine duly appeared, and as Sam poured two glasses the screen flickered to life. Several nearby passengers fixed on headsets to listen to the soundtrack, while others settled back to sleep. In the gloom, it was as though they were marooned alone on a desert island.

'We'll talk,' Sam said quietly. 'I'll do a Vivienne and reveal all!'

'I already know a little bit,' Jenna confessed, taking a sip of wine. 'Vivienne told me your mother died when you were a teenager and you split with your father.'

'Did she tell you that we buried the hatchet several years later and that now my father, stepmother Susan and I have a great relationship?'

Jenna shook her head. 'She only gave me a broad outline. What does your father do?'

'He's a . . . businessman,' Sam told her.

'And what did you do when you left Australia?'

'I bummed around the Far East. At times it was traumatic, so I was forced to grow up fast, but in retrospect the experience was extremely beneficial. Until then I'd led a pampered existence. Everything I'd ever wanted had been handed to me on a silver platter, because my father is rich. As a consequence I was self-centred and self-obsessed. My reaction to my father's second marriage was typical of a spoiled kid. I never tried to put myself in his shoes, and imagine how lonely he felt when my mother died, all I cared about was *my* feelings! One of my reasons for chucking university and leaving home was to make my father suffer. At one stage I was tempted to join the Foreign Legion, but that did seem rather extreme!' Sam grinned at the memory. 'So I wandered through Malaysia and Thailand and met some fascinating characters who taught me there was more to life than acquiring wealth.'

'Like who?' she asked, wishing now she had had the opportunity to travel in her youth. Yet the opportunity had been there, if she had chosen to take it, but instead she had rushed into an early marriage.

'A Vietnamese guy. He was well educated and spoke several languages, part of his time had been spent in France. Now he was homeless, living rough like me. I asked him what he missed from his former life, expecting him to quote fast cars or fine houses, but he said he missed very little. He pointed out that his pleasures in the past had been manmade and costly, but now they came free, gifts of nature.'

'What do you mean?' Jenna queried.

Sam took a mouthful of wine. 'Like the colours of the sunset. I've never known anyone so alert to the sheer magic of simple things. We'd go for a walk and he'd be pointing out the slant of sunshine through the trees, the military march of black ants across a fallen branch, the symmetry of a cluster of flowers. I began to take photographs to record this bounty of nature. I'd snap a single leaf or an entire landscape, and gradually I moved on to people.' He smiled. 'Some of the older Asians believe a photograph takes away part of your soul, so they refused to allow me and my camera anywhere near. I learnt to be unobtrusive, which helped when I arrived in Vietnam.'

'Why did you go there?'

'My friend was desperate to trace his family, so I went along on the offchance I could help.'

'Wasn't it very dangerous?' asked Jenna, frowning.

'It was. The hostilities, as such, were supposed to be over, but the country was in turmoil. However, I was too conspicuous to stay for long. You don't find many Vietnamese over six feet tall!'

'What happened to your friend?'

Sam's expression became grave. 'I don't know. When I realised my presence was proving to be a liability, I said I must leave. He understood. We parted and I never saw him again. When I returned home I sold some of my pictures to raise money to support myself.'

'You didn't go back to your family?'

He shook his head. 'Although I was older and a bit wiser, I still couldn't face the prospect of sharing the family home with a stepmother. My sisters had accepted her in total, so they couldn't understand my reluctance to make amends. My father came to see me, but I was still too pigheaded to apologise in full. My photographs were proving to be moneyspinners, so . . .'

'They won awards?' Jenna put in.

He rubbed his jaw thoughtfully. 'Yes, they were good.' There was no braggadocio about him, it was a mere statement of fact. 'I rapidly gained something of a reputation and was offered a job as a television cameraman. After a spell of training and some local work, I began volunteering for the distant assignments no one else wanted.'

'Why?'

'Because I had no ties and because the travel bug had bitten me.' He arched a mocking brow. 'And because I was in my early twenties and saw myself as Superman Mark Two, I suspect!'

Jenna laughed. 'You were a daredevil?'

There was a pause as he refilled their glasses, then he took hold of her hand, rubbing the ball of his thumb across her palm.

'I'd been a wild kid, but my mother's death pushed me further off the rails. I wouldn't describe it as a death wish, I enjoyed life too much for that, but danger became an aphrodisiac. That's partly why I went to Vietnam, just for the sheer hell of it! I became a specialist in filming danger, diving into war-torn countries like a kid into chocolate cake. I buried all the normal feelings for self-preservation and everyone began to admire me because I was "cool".'

'Where did you go?' she asked.

'The Lebanon, banana republics, Afghanistan, Northern Ireland.' Sam twitched his shoulders. 'Any place where the bullets flew and bombs left huge craters in the hillsides. I had a great mate, another cameraman, a guy called Trevor. We were two of a kind, except that he had a wife and family back home. We worked together for several years, taking more and more risks. Then we landed in some god-awful South American country.' He gave a long-drawn-out sigh. 'We'd had to bribe our way across no man's land and were tucking in behind a derelict building when a stray bullet came out of nowhere. Just one, but Trevor stopped it. His life was over. God, it was awful! When I returned to Sydney I went to see his widow. She was furious—

furious with Trevor for dying and furious with me for encouraging him.' Sam shook his head in slow disbelief. 'Some of the things she said that night! Anyway, it brought me to my senses. I stopped taking chances for no reason at all, and I realised life was precious.'

'What did you do next?' Jenna asked.

The sweep of his thumb across her palm lessened its pressure.

'I packed in news-reporting. I made peace with my father and his wife, and began to rethink my future. I'd saved a healthy sum of money from my "Dangerous Dan" episode.' He gave a self-deprecating grin. 'So I decided to have a shot at making a film about the flora and fauna in the Northern Territory, what we Australians call "The Top End". It's very quiet up there. They reckon there's about .08 people to the square kilometre, and my God, it seems like an overstatement at times!'

Jenna raised her brows. 'Did you make the film alone?'

'No. I had some help from the television company I'd worked for, they provided additional crew and editing facilities, that kind of thing. Once I took a girl up into the Top End with me. She was supposed to be my sound assistant.' Sam had a mouthful of wine and wiped his lips with the back of his hand, grinning wickedly. 'We shared the same sleeping bag.'

'I thought you might,' she quipped, but not without a twinge of pique.

'But she wasn't interested.'

'Not interested in you and your sleeping bag?' Jenna said archly.

His thumb hesitated on her palm, then resumed its circling. 'She was interested in *that*! But she was a dead loss as far as anything else was concerned. She would click her fingers all day long to pop songs on her radio, she couldn't give a damn about our surroundings. Once

I called her out to see a wonderful sunset and she took so long fixing her face that it was dark when she appeared!' He groaned. 'And her clothes! I've always considered clothes to be just a means of not getting arrested, but she had to have everything strung up on hangers in the tent so they wouldn't get creased.' He wiped a hand across his brow to remove imaginary sweat. 'Was she a pain!'

'So how many wildlife documentaries have you done?' asked Jenna.

He grew thoughtful. 'Five, so far. The last concerned the underwater life around the Barrier Reef and the next will be made in the Scottish Highlands. I've arranged most of my film notes for that, I did quite a useful amount in Paris.'

'You worked in Paris?' she said in surprise.

'Yes, I write everything down, do my research, then I know . . .'

'So you weren't writing an article about Vivienne?'

'No! She doesn't interest me. Why should you . . .?' He stopped suddenly and leant forward to dab a fingertip into the dimple on her chin. 'Don't say you believed me when I said I'd write about her?' He was smiling broadly.

Jenna's thick lashes swept downwards. 'I did,' she confessed, then her voice grew firmer. 'You sounded definite.'

'But you'd hurt me, honeybunch. You'd struck the first blow so I had to retaliate, but it was only a sham.'

She pouted. 'I never know where I am with you.'

'Good, I don't want to be too predictable,' he grinned, leaning forward to place a kiss where his finger had been.

Sydney was warm, very warm at six o'clock in the morning. Jenna slung her coat over her arm, hitched up her duffle-bag and held tightly on to Christopher's hand, propelling him after Sam through the airport.

'It's like England!' she exclaimed when the taxi brought them into the outskirts of the city, for the factories, the shops, the houses, were replicas of those back home. 'We've flown all this way and it's exactly like England!'

'What did you expect, kangaroos on every corner?' Sam teased.

Christopher bounced up and down on Jenna's knees. 'Kanga, kanga, roo, roo,' he burbled happily, going off into a chant.

At Singapore he had snapped back to life and ever since had sparkled with such brilliance that Jenna was losing patience with his never-ending vitality. Sam had managed to grab an hour or two of sleep, but she had never settled again, and now her head was fuzzy and she was stale, stale, *stale*. If only her son would show signs of a little tiredness too, but instead he was alert, watching from the car window, pointing out the sights to 'Teddy-daddy'.

'I'll see you settled in your hotel and then I'll be off.' Sam checked his sports watch. 'I'm not too sure when the first ferry leaves for Manly, but I can always have a bite of breakfast to pass the time.'

Jenna's brow wrinkled. 'Aren't you staying with us?' Blithely she had presumed they would be together for the whole assignment, but had asked no questions about Sam's arrangements back at the office and now realised she had taken too much for granted. A tiny feeling of disappointment flickered and flamed. 'What's at Manly?' she asked. 'And where is it?'

He stretched, pulling off his sweater over his head to reveal a chalk-blue short-sleeved shirt and tanned forearms, gilded with golden hair. 'Manly is a holiday centre on the far side of the harbour from Sydney. I have a house there.' He tucked his shirt into his jeans, lifting first one hip, then the other.

'Is it a long way?'

Jenna didn't want him to leave her. She needed Sam. She would be miserable on her own, even with Christopher for company. There were two days to kill before she could contact Vivienne who was scheduled to arrive the following day, and how could she exist all that time without Sam?

He raked back his hair. 'Manly's half an hour away by ferry, go by hydrofoil and it's even quicker. Or you can drive over the Harbour Bridge.' He grinned at the vulnerability paling her cheeks. 'Don't worry, honeybunch, I shan't be far away.'

'Kangaroo!' Christopher interrupted loudly, leaping up and down with excitement as he pointed to a billboard advertising beer which, sure enough, featured a large brown kangaroo.

Everyone laughed.

The hotel was a soaring tower block in the heart of the city, a tree-filled park to one side, a glimpse of the blue waters of the harbour on the other. Sam took Christopher off to find the loo while Jenna checked in.

'I'm afraid we're overbooked, madam,' the desk clerk said, but when her face fell, he added quickly, 'So we've given you a suite at the same daily rate.'

'Thank you.' She leant against the counter in relief. Lack of sleep was making her lightheaded and she would have said thank you to a broom cupboard, just so long as she could lie down full-length and close her eyes.

She had filled in the necessary forms and taken possession of her key when Sam appeared beside her, Christopher in his arms.

'All set, honeybunch?' he asked.

'I didn't realise your husband was with you,' the desk clerk apologised, rechecking the registration form.

'I'm a widow,' Jenna started to explain.

'Daddy Sam!' yelled Christopher, punching a fist into Sam's collarbone.

'I'm not staying here,' said Sam, all at the same time.

The desk clerk's eyes grew round as saucers, and Jenna would not have been surprised if they had started to spin like Catherine wheels, so great was his confusion. 'Er ... I'll ask the porter to take up your luggage,' he muttered, nonplussed by the curious ménage à trois he imagined before him.

The suite consisted of two rooms, one with a double bed, one with a single, plus a separate shower and bathroom, all in appealing shades of pale gold, caramel and cream. There was a fridge, colour television, kettle accompanied by tea and coffee, and a writing desk with vast supplies of stationery. Everything she needed.

'Leave that alone!' snapped Jenna with a tiny burst of temper as Christopher squatted down to examine an electric plug. She slapped his hand. 'It's bedtime,' she explained, feeling guilty because he was on the brink of tears, bottom lip trembling at her unexpected anger. She followed his eyes to the window where sunshine streamed in through the sheer white net curtains. 'I know it's daylight, but we've had a long journey and everyone's tired.'

'Except your son,' Sam said wryly, lounging in the doorway between the two rooms.

Even Sam was weary, Jenna realised, for beneath his tan his face was drawn, dark rings around his eyes.

'If you'd like to stay here until the ferry opens up, please do,' she offered. 'I'm taking Christopher into the double bed with me, so let's hope he'll cotton on to the fact that now is the time to sleep. The single bedroom is free.'

Sam yawned, stretching out his arms. 'Thanks, I'll stay for an hour or so. I'm just about ready to drop.'

When he had disappeared she washed Christopher and popped him into his sleepsuit before taking a quick shower and pulling on her baby doll pyjamas. Closing the heavy curtains against the sunlight, she drew the little boy into bed.

'Go to sleep, you monster,' she pleaded as he banged his hands flat on the counterpane in some jungle beat. He began to chant 'Roo, roo' in discord.

Jenna ignored him, feeling certain he must quieten down soon. His mumbles had faded into the middle distance when a determined finger prised open her eyelid, dragging her back from the edge of sleep.

'Mummy sing a song,' he requested. She muttered something unfit for his ears, but rolled over and obligingly stumbled her way through an off-key lullaby. 'Again,' he insisted, smiling with pleasure as she finished.

'No. Mummy's tired—lie down.'

Making a grab for the small wriggling body, she tucked him in beside her beneath the covers, but now the little boy had decided she was playing some kind of game.

'Do it again,' he said jauntily, romping out of bed to sit astride her.

'Christopher, get back in here and go to sleep,' she instructed, but she was too lethargic to fire her words with the necessary force and they fell upon stony ground. He laughed, frolicking over the blankets. Jenna had wilted, she had no hidden reserves of strength. 'Go to sleep,' she pleaded, her eyelids closing of their own accord.

Dimly she heard a door open, then the small squirming body was yanked away.

'Right, Boy Wonder, you come with me and leave your mummy in peace,' said Sam.

She fell asleep.


Jenna awoke with a start, eyes springing open wide. The room was gloomy, though sunlight still showed in a golden strip beneath the curtains. She held herself taut.

Far below came the murmur of city traffic, but in the room the only noise was the soft breathing of the man stretched out beside her on top of the bedclothes. A muscled arm lay across her chest, pinning her down. Sam was sound asleep, lying on his stomach with his head towards her, his long body fitted into her curves and hollows. His shoulders and back were naked, the tanned skin gleaming in the subdued light. Her eyes travelled cautiously downwards. He was wearing his jeans, thank goodness. She would not have been surprised if Sam had come naked into her bed like those imaginary lovers he had mentioned. But whatever his reason for being there, it was not as a lover; he had been far too drained by the long journey for such exuberance.

How long had she been asleep? Searching carefully for her watch on the bedside table, Jenna saw it was mid-afternoon. No sound came from the other room, the door was closed, and she concluded that Christopher had finally succumbed and was now catching up on some of the sleep he had missed. In an odd way the heavy warmth of Sam against her was satisfying, and as it seemed unfair to leap up and disturb his rest, she relaxed against him, falling into a voluptuous bliss. She felt she could purr. She was at peace, refreshed and secure, her son asleep in the next room, and Sam . . .

Strands of her hair were straggled across his shoulder and gently she picked them free, her fingers straying to caress him. He stirred, moving closer in his sleep, and after a moment, when his breathing remained rhythmic, Jenna grew brave. Embarking on a cautious voyage, she touched the thick hair which had fallen across his brow, brushing it aside and revelling in the vital spring with which it pushed against her fingers. He was not so blond after all, she decided. The roots of his hair were dark, which explained the colour of the rough stubble on his jaw; months of sun and sea-water must have

bleached the ends of his hair far paler than its natural
shade. Carefully she placed her hand on the top of his
spine, sliding it down along the smooth furrow at a
slow pace. She had had no idea Sam was so muscular.
True, he had loomed large in his sweater and sheepskin
coat, but the bunched muscles across his shoulders
resembled well-developed boulders. He had mentioned
long spells swimming underwater with a snorkel as he
filmed the coral gardens of the Barrier Reef and his
muscles must have been honed to perfection with the
exercise.

Unable to leave him alone, her fingers were
irresistibly drawn to caress him again, this time to trace
the outline of his nose. Too bony to be handsome, it
was a statement of an inborn arrogance, of someone
who was his own man, who rarely worried about the
impression he might make on other people. Jenna's
fingers trickled downwards to press against the budding
softness of his lips when, without warning, his mouth
opened and she was captured. With sleep-softened lips
Sam kissed her fingers before she grabbed them free.

'Been enjoying yourself, honeybunch?' he asked, and
his arm tightened across her, holding her in position. 'I
was waiting for you to start unzipping my jeans.'

Jenna flushed bright scarlet. 'I didn't want to wake
you, and I couldn't move, so . . .' she flustered.

'So you thought you'd reconnoitre?' He was witty,
mocking, tender, all at the same time. He looked
gravely at the face he adored. 'We belong together,
Jenna, you and I,' he murmured, sliding beneath the
covers to join her, but when she made as if to swing
free, he buried his face in her neck. 'Stop fighting,' he
implored, raising brown eyes to hers. 'I'm not going to
hurt you. I love and I need you—*now*!'

A sprinkle of stars burst over her. 'You can't!' she
gasped.

Sam moved closer, one of his legs nudging between

hers. 'I can and I do,' he said fiercely. 'God, can't you *feel* how much I need you?'

'But I don't need you.' It rang hopelessly false, but there was nothing she could do about it. With an effort she added, 'And I don't love you, either.'

In anger Sam made a pseudo-bite at her throat. 'Then why the hell are you as aroused by me as I am by you?' he demanded.

'I'm not,' she denied weakly.

Sam pushed himself up and roughly ripped open the buttons of her pyjama top. 'Jenna!' He cupped her breasts in both hands, stroking his fingertips across the rosy jutting pinnacles. 'Why, in God's name, are you in this state if you don't want us to make love?'

He bent to kiss her, his lips lighting a fire over which she had no control. She was in flames, her breasts straining to fill his palms, their peaks so tight they ached. Sam's mouth was everywhere, teasing and tormenting, nibbling at her ears, her shoulders. His kisses moved lower to the creamy swollen curves and she was lost, writhing beneath his weight, running her fingers through his hair, across the hard muscles of his back, clutching wildly, repeating his name over and over. His mouth was as warmly erotic on her breast as it had been on her thumb and she found her hips sliding against his with a passion she did not dare to understand.

'Jenna, my darling, my love,' Sam groaned, and slithered his hand down between their two bodies.

'Don't!' Her voice cracked and the note of desperation made him pause. Like a switch being flipped her desire fled. Her head cleared and now she lay in his arms like a wooden doll.

Sam took several harsh breaths, fighting for control, and when he succeeded he slid an arm around her shoulders.

'Tell me what's the matter,' he said gently, but she lay

there, stiff and unyielding, desperately unhappy.

She stared up at the ceiling for what seemed to be for ever. There was a sharp intake of breath and then she said in a voice devoid of all emotion, 'It's no use Sam, I'm frigid.'

## CHAPTER SEVEN

SAM swore loud and long, and in remarkable detail, then he rubbed his nose against her cheek and sighed. 'Don't talk such utter nonsense.'

'It isn't nonsense!' Words were sticking in Jenna's throat, but she ripped them free. 'I was married for six years and in all that time I never once enoyed . . . sex.' She flicked a disdainful hand, separating herself from him inch by painful inch. 'With you I admit the . . . the foreplay, as you call it, is exciting, but I don't want to go any further.' There was a sob in her voice. 'I daren't. If we make love you'll be disappointed and . . . and . . .' She swallowed hard, pushing her head into the pillow as a teardrop rolled down her cheek. 'And you'll take away my self-respect. I need that, I couldn't bear for you to despise me.' She tried to imagine the situation from his point of view. 'You can easily find another girl, Sam, one who's capable of satisfying you. You're a sensual man, you need a sensual woman. I'm not made like that. I'm no good for you.' She closed her eyes, but scenes from the past, scenes of herself and Edward, were too vivid, and she sat up abruptly, fastening her pyjamas and wiping away her tears with the back of her hand. 'How did you come to be in my bed in the first place?' she demanded.

Sam laced his hands behind his head and watched her withdrawal, noting the tension which had tightened her features, draining her complexion to porcelain-pale.

'Christopher and I had half an hour's hectic fun and then he fell asleep. I was afraid if I slept too, I might fling out an arm unawares and knock him out cold, so I came through here. You were curled up on one side of

147

the bed, leaving plenty of room, and I lay down, intending it to be only for a few minutes, and ...' his full mouth lurched, 'I only woke when you started making advances. You're wrong on both counts, Jenna. You *are* good for me and you are sensual. You enjoyed touching me.' He wasn't asking, he was telling her. 'Don't forget I've seen you and Christopher together. You derive tremendous satisfaction from playing with him, the feel of his body in your arms, his cheek rubbing against yours.'

'That's different,' she cut in briskly, swinging her legs to climb out of bed.

He caught hold of her hand, kissing its palm as he surreptitiously observed her. 'No, it's not. Sensuality doesn't merely relate to sexual pleasures, it concerns the five senses—touch, sight, hearing, smell and taste. Kids know what it's all about, but adults often become so "civilised" they forget the delight of jelly squelching between your fingers, or watching a feather float on an air spiral, or the satisfying "plop" a tennis ball makes when it hits water.'

There was a tearing sound from the other room, and Sam joined Jenna in her leap for the door.

'Or the slow rip of paper as you tear a page from the telephone directory,' he drawled.

Christopher was stretched out on the carpet surrounded by his bounty—notepaper and envelopes, a bible, some teabags, menu cards and the telephone directory, now minus several pages.

'What am I raising—a juvenile delinquent?' Jenna exclaimed, rushing forward to rescue the book before it suffered further damage.

Slouched against the door, Sam grinned. 'A young man's bound to become bored if his mother's entertaining a gentleman in bed and there's no one to talk to.'

'Sam!' she remonstrated, visualising her son spreading

details of the two of them in bed together. She spun to glare at the little boy. 'Don't you dare do that again!'

Tears started in his baby-blue eyes.

'Don't cry,' she implored, gathering him up against her. 'You'll disturb the people in the next room.' A few cuddles and she was successful in stopping the tears before they started. 'How about you and me going for a walk in the park?'

Christopher nodded. It struck Jenna that being in a strange city, in a hotel with a small boy, had its share of pitfalls.

Sam rubbed his jaw thoughtfully and when he said, 'Suppose you check out of here and we all go to Manly?' she realised he was tuned into the same wavelength. 'My house has a backyard, all enclosed, where Chris can play and the couple next door, Marge and Barry, have young children too, so it won't matter if he yells now and then.' He tossed a glance around the room. 'He'll be bored stiff, cooped up here. The minute you turn your back he'll start clambering up the curtains or dismantling the television.'

'Stop it, you're giving him ideas,' she pleaded, for her son was listening, ears pricked.

Sam glanced across at her. 'I have ample space and . . .' he paused, stroking his fingertips across the naked hairiness of his chest to describe a slow circle, 'and if you're worried I might crawl into your bed again, forget it. I don't gatecrash, I only come by invitation.'

They made their way on to the upper deck as the ferryboat eased off the Circular Quay. The view was breathtaking. To their left was the coathanger ironwork of the Harbour Bridge, while to the right Bennelong Point projected into the water, the white outline of the Opera House rising in a series of elegant pinnacles against china-blue sky.

'Sydney Harbour is much larger than I imagined, it

must stretch for miles,' Jenna exclaimed, as the ferry
chugged along in the warm sunshine, past Fort
Dennison, which Sam explained had once been an
island prison. Spread around them, the harbour was a
dazzling blue counterpane, patched with triangular sails
of white and rainbow colours. On wooded hillsides
there were glimpses of fine houses and swimming pools,
while tiny bays provided sheltered anchorage for
bobbing yachts.

'I've never seen so many boats,' she smiled.

'This is nothing, you should be here for the start of
the Sydney to Hobart Yacht Race,' said Sam, grinning
at her pleasure, for in her excitement she was clutching
at the rail. 'There's hardly a spare inch of water,
anything that floats is on the harbour that day—luxury
ocean-going sloops, windsurfers, youngsters in clapped
out dinghies, the Navy. You name it, it's here.' He
shook his head in amused patriotic pride. 'I swear some
folk would sail in bathtubs if they could. No one cares
what their craft looks like, so long as they're here. The
racing boats are magnificent, hulls gleaming like
polished ebony, all in tiptop condition. When the
starting gun is fired, if the weather is right, the
spinnakers bloom like huge exotic flowers—violet,
lemon, green, red and white striped. It's so beautiful it
brings a lump to your throat. I reckon boats are one of
the few manmade inventions which *do* add to a scene.'

'Do you sail?' asked Jenna, as he hoisted Christopher
up on to his shoulders to give him a better vantage
point.

'How could you live in Sydney and not sail?' he
countered. 'This is an outdoor city with a great climate.
There are thirty-four beaches within easy reach. Manly
has two, a harbour beach at the wharf where we land,
and an ocean beach.'

'And where is your house?'

'At the far end of the ocean beach. I bought it as an

investment and as a base between filming excursions. Things are fine now with my stepmother, but I'm too long in the tooth to be living at home.'

'You need your independence, like me,' Jenna said pointedly, then when she saw his tightlipped response, rather wished she hadn't.

On the surface all was amiable, but their relationship had shifted, only slightly, but it was a shift capable of bringing a shiver to her spine despite the warmth of the overhead sun. Sam had retreated, and although her head told her that was what she wanted, her heart stubbornly insisted otherwise. The invisible lasso had loosened a notch, leaving her emotions somewhat battered and her mind adrift.

She swung from him, resting her elbows against the rail to inspect her legs. How pale they were! Both she and Christopher were in tee-shirts and shorts; his navy with a white Mickey Mouse on his chest, hers in clover-pink with a lilac trim. The sea breeze lifted her hair from her face and Jenna stretched, freezing mid-frame, breasts tilted provocatively, when a swarthy youth on the far side of the deck winked. But the gesture held no threat, it was merely one human being appreciating another, and she relaxed, allowing him a fraction of a grin before turning back to Sam's side. Was it the euphoric effect of sun and sea that made her triumphant to be young, female and pretty enough to draw complimentary glances? Jenna did not know, but lightheartedly she linked her arm through Sam's and nestled her head against the thrust of his shoulder.

'What's that for?' he asked, sternly suspicious at the unexpected caress.

'Because I like you.'

Beneath the short sleeve, his arm was firm and brown, and Jenna rubbed her lips gently, opening her mouth to touch his skin with the tip of her tongue. The flesh was warm, tasting slightly of salt.

'Mmm, nice,' she murmured, smiling up at him through her lashes.

A muscle leapt in his jaw. 'Jenna,' he growled in a low warning voice, 'I'm living on a knife edge as it is. For God's sake, don't start arousing me on purpose.'

'I'm not!'

'You are! You're arousing me and yourself, but don't start something you have no intention of finishing,' he hurled in a fierce undertone, glaring at the other passengers as though he wished them in hell. 'You've told me where we stand, so *leave it at that!*'

His warning was vicious enough to quell any response, and Jenna spun away. The cold anger in his eyes made her suspect World War Three had started and it was all her fault! Gathering up her tattered pride, she studied the shoreline, grateful that Christopher, at least, was his usual irrepressible self, pointing a chubby finger at the procession of passing boats and asking, 'What's that, what's that?'

By the time they reached his house, Sam had recovered his composure and took them on a tour, exhibiting not a little pride, all justifiable. His home was attractive; upstairs there were three bedrooms and two bathrooms, and downstairs a large kitchen-cum-dining room, lounge and rumpus room. A double garage was attached, with an open spread of lawn at the front of the house and a fenced-in garden to the rear.

'This is where I spend most of my time,' he told her, opening the door to the rumpus room. He indicated the floor-to-ceiling bookshelves, the filing cabinets, the bleached pine desk. 'All my preparatory work is done at home whenever possible. We'll keep this out of bounds to young Christopher.'

Jenna nodded agreement, for the lower shelves were packed with loose-leaf files which she knew could provide her son with many happy hours!

'I only have the bare essentials,' Sam grinned when they entered the lounge. 'No collections of pot dogs or priceless Ming china, so you, young man, can do your damnedest!' He swung Christopher into the air, making him crow with delight.

'Don't worry, I'll keep him under control,' Jenna put in, for although simply furnished the lounge was comfortable, with calfskin and sheepskin rugs thrown over the sanded floor, a huge squashy sofa and chairs in tan leather, creamy woven floor cushions and a variety of pot plants. The personal touches were few; a wicker lobster pot that housed magazines, a stereo and television, both out of reach of an active two-year-old, and some brass gongs fixed high. One wall was of rough-hewed stone, mint-green ivies trailing profusely from hidden crevices, and another was of glass, where sliding patio doors led on to a paved area with the back garden beyond.

When Christopher sidled over to poke a curious finger at the magazines, Sam bent to him.

'We'll establish ground rules now,' he said sternly, and Christopher's eyes became plate-sized. 'If you touch that you get a smacked bottom, like this.' He gave the little boy a tap on the backside. 'Understand?'

'Yes,' whispered Christopher, edging away, suddenly in awe. He popped his thumb in his mouth and sucked furiously for a minute, considering the warning. 'Yes, Daddy Sam.' He gazed up at the man towering above him, but when Sam winked his face broke into a smile of relief and he held out his arms. 'Up,' he demanded.

Chuckling, Sam lifted the toddler. He had embarked on an explanation of how, if Christopher behaved himself, all kinds of treats could fall his way, when there was a knock at the back door. He strode through to the kitchen, Jenna following.

'Hi there, sugar plum,' a voice laughed, and a vivacious young woman with short dark hair bounced

in. She was in tennis gear, and from the look of her trim
athletic build, Jenna deduced she would be an agile
opponent on the far side of the net.

'I thought I saw you arrive, Sam.' She stood on tiptoe
to plant a hearty kiss on his cheek. 'And who's this?'
she asked, smiling at Christopher. 'What a gorgeous
little girl!'

'Me boy,' he said indignantly.

Jenna laughed. 'That's my son, Christopher. I know
his hair is on the long side, but every time I take him to
the barber's he raises the roof, so I stretch out the space
between visits as far as I can.'

'Marge, this is Jenna Devine, plus son. Jenna, this is
Marge Brown from next door,' said Sam by way of
introduction. 'Jenna's staying here for a week or so.
She's flown over from England to interview Vivienne
Valdis for her newspaper.'

Looking suitably impressed, Marge greeted her
cheerfully. 'My two girls will love having a toddler
around,' she said, unable to take her eyes off
Christopher's angelic appearance. 'Sarah's ten, so she's
sensible, but I suspect Beth, who's six, will treat him
like a toy and haul him around all over the place.' With
an effort she abandoned the little boy's charms and
turned to Sam. 'Are you all right for food? I can let you
have some milk and bread to tide you over.'

'Marge, quit the mothering!' Sam joked. He checked
his watch. 'There's an hour before the supermarket
closes, so Jenna and I will drive over and stock up.'

'Don't fix a meal for this evening,' his neighbour
ordered. 'We're having a barbecue and Barry can easily
thrown in a few more steaks.'

Sam grinned at Jenna. 'Okay?' he asked.

'Yes, please.'

A delicious smell of sizzling meat hung on the balmy air
when the three of them made their way into next-door's

garden that evening. Two little girls were dancing up and down in giggling anticipation.

'Who's that?' Christopher demanded, pulling at Jenna's trouser leg.

'I'm Sarah,' the bigger one said.

'And I'm Beth.'

He swivelled to stare wide-eyed at a large man with crinkly brown hair who was tending a charcoal barbecue on the patio. 'Who's that?'

'That's my daddy,' said Sarah.

Christopher grinned up at Sam as if to claim him as his daddy, but mercifully kept quiet.

Sarah held out her hand to him. 'We've got a kitten too, would you like to see it?' Taking charge, she led him away with Beth dancing around.

The large man smiled, wiping his hand on his navy and white apron before offering it to Jenna. 'I'm Barry. Welcome to Australia.'

'Thanks, it's lovely to be here.' She peered towards the grill where a selection of steaks, sausages and chicken drumsticks were cooking above hotly glowing embers. 'Those look gorgeous.'

Sam and Barry exchanged greetings, giving a mutual cheer when Marge appeared carrying two foaming tankards.

'Great stuff,' grinned Sam, wiping the froth from his lips. 'Try some, Jenna, it's streets ahead of that warmed-up cold tea they pass off as beer in England!' Laughing, he sidestepped to deflect her elbow-dig of mock anger.

'Would you like beer, or do you prefer wine?' Marge asked.

'Wine, please.'

'What do you think of our Australian vintages?' Barry enquired, turning over the steaks with long metal tongs.

'Wonderful, I'm becoming an addict.' Jenna took a

sip from the glass Marge had provided and her tastebuds leapt with delight. As the others exchanged news, she smiled to herself. The evening was a tranquil golden time, the sky daubed with flame and scarlet, while at the far end of the garden a languid breeze waltzed with the pines, lifting their branches and scenting the warm air. She gave a soft sigh of pleasure.

Marge placed a vast bowl of salad on the plank table. 'Told you they'd get on like a house on fire,' she said, nodding towards the kitchen where there was the laughter of happy children. 'The girls are on school holidays at the moment, so Christopher is a godsend. He'll stop them getting bored. Shunt him round here whenever you like.' She grinned at her husband. 'I've been feeling broody of late, so having a little one to cuddle will help to satisfy the urge.'

'It had better,' Barry said in horror. 'Two kids are enough for anyone.'

'Spoilsport,' grinned Sam.

Jenna's tastebuds leapt again later, for the barbecued steaks melted in her mouth, and the meal had to be one of the most delicious she had ever tasted. Everyone was relaxed, enjoying the mellow calm of the Antipodean evening, and eating heartily. Even Christopher had a second helping, though his appetite was often pernickety, and then he embarrassed her by spooning up the Pavlova Marge produced and promptly demanding more.

Sam winked at the little boy. 'I told you you'd like it!'

When everyone had finished eating, Sarah and Beth took Christopher off again and the adults sat around the table, drinking more wine and beer in a leisurely fashion, and talking. The end of the evening arrived all too soon, but the children were noticeably flagging and when Christopher came to sit on Jenna's knee and suck his thumb, his silver-white head lolling against her, it was time to go.

'Bedtime,' Sam decreed, and there was a burst of cheery farewells, the little girls asking if Christopher could play in the morning, while Marge promised another barbecue, 'real soon'.

Jenna washed and undressed her son at speed, but his eyelids had closed before she tucked him up in the tiny bedroom. Sam had suggested a nightcap, so afterwards she went downstairs, but now that they were alone she was conscious of a sensation of stiff constraint which had not existed earlier. Talking over the evening, they were like two actors repeating lines, and it was a relief when her glass was empty and she could make a hasty retreat. Sam's 'goodnight' was cursory. He made no attempt to bestow a kiss similar to the one he had given Marge, and when he came upstairs Jenna heard him shut his bedroom door with such definition that she knew any fears, or hopes, of him coming out again before morning were groundless.

His attitude had not changed at breakfast. True, he was the genial host, telling her a little of Manly's history and about the area in general, but he was still intent on keeping himself to himself. If his outspoken comments had dismayed her in the past, now Jenna longed for one flash of impish humour, but none was forthcoming. She was not surprised when he asked if she was capable of entertaining herself that day.

'I have some business in the city,' he explained. 'I must finalise the Barrier Reef documentary. When I left, I left in a hurry, so one or two matters are pending, and also I'm expected to report my outline for the Scottish film to the powers that be.'

'Go ahead, I'll be fine,' she assured him, fighting down a surge of unreasonable resentment. 'I'll take Christopher to the beach for a picnic, and perhaps Sarah and Beth will come, too.'

The girls were delighted at the idea, and as Sam roared off in a battered red sports car he had produced from the garage, Jenna made her way towards the bay, Christopher toddling before her, each hand tightly clasped by an attentive female. First they visited the Corso, a picturesque boulevard lined with shops, which straddled the narrow peninsula, linking the harbour to the ocean beach. When Jenna had bought a sun-hat, and bucket and spade for her son, they headed for the shore. In minutes the children were happily engrossed in building sandcastles, and she stripped off shirt and shorts to stretch out in her bikini. Tomorrow she would contact Vivienne and arrange a further meeting. Already Marge had offered to look after Christopher, so the working side of her life was taken care of, but that still left her relationship with Sam . . .

Idly running grains of sand through her fingers, Jenna wondered how she could repair matters between them. Sam was hurt and angry, she knew that. Did he imagine she was lying to him? Perhaps he considered she was not giving him the true reason for rebuffing his advances? He had seemed unconvinced by her explanation that her own shortcomings were the cause of her resistance to his lovemaking. Blue eyes thoughtful, she rubbed the sand between her fingertips. It was imperative she make him understand *he* was not at fault. Her expression grew misty. In her opinion Sam had few faults, he was all she could desire—an amusing, caring companion. Even his attitude towards Christopher was pleasing, with its blend of uncomplicated pleasure, interspersed with discipline.

Jenna sat upright, bending her legs to rest her chin on her knees as she stared out at the ocean. She could not be *in love* with Sam, could she? Her heart stopped beating as she hastily marshalled the reasons why it didn't make sense. They had only known each other for a matter of weeks. Her plans for the future were fiercely independent. She had no need for a man, and no need for lovemaking, or had she . . .? Her toes curled into the sand. Sam had taught her that touching and kissing could equal pleasure, deep pleasure. He had taught her more in weeks than Edward had ever done in years. Edward! Her stomach plunged sickeningly. The one way to make Sam understand her inhibitions would be to explain about Edward.

To the world at large, or so she had presumed until Maggi's acerbic comments, she and Edward had had the appearance of being a happily married couple. Her interest in his career had bridged the gap in their ages, and there had always been enough happening outside their home to bolster the conversation within it. But though their mutual fascination with politics had played a major part in bringing them together, a successful marriage needed more. To her inexperienced eye, Edward had been the courteous sophisticate, and when, during their courtship, he had restricted his embraces to a nightly kiss, she had understood. Secretly she was impressed by his dignity and self-control. Edward preferred to do everything 'properly'; he never said so, but she knew.

When their marital lovemaking first showed signs of being torpid, she had rushed to blame herself. Edward was a man of the world, she was an awkward ingénue. And yet, although her budding realisation that something was wrong rapidly blossomed into frantic dismay, Edward seemed immune to any misgivings. His career meant he frequently travelled the hundreds of miles between London and Manchester and though, at first, Jenna commuted with him, she soon grasped that he did not wish her to be his constant companion. He preferred to continue his previous lifestyle, though when he produced her at dinner parties or election rallies, he would gaze upon her with fond delight as though she was his favourite doll. And a doll was the sum total of all he needed; a living breathing woman with physical requirements made him uneasy.

Jenna's immature ego took a terrible pounding.
Thanks to her husband's disregard, her self-confidence
as a desirable woman gradually drained away. Her self-
esteem shrivelled. When she discovered spontaneous
displays of affection made him cringe, she suppressed
her natural urges. Over the years her feelings had
fluctuated, for Edward had treated her amiably,
choosing to ignore any hint that his young bride was
less than happy. There had been bitterness, self-
searching, secret nights of tearful yearning, spells of
black hatred, more mature intervals of cynical
acceptance. Finally Jenna had grown impatient with
herself. Edward was not going to change at his time of
life. She channelled her energies into her writing with a
success which, ironically, delighted her husband, but as
time passed she realised a career would not be
fulfilment enough. She needed someone to love, and if
Edward rejected her affection then she would have a
child—a child would love her!

Edward's illness had come as a complete shock,
overturning her secret plans for the future and throwing
her emotions into a state of chaos. What did she do
now? She felt guilty because their marriage had not
been a success—and yet in Edward's view it was all he
desired. With a characteristic need for organisation, he
had demanded that the doctor tell him the worst, plus
time-scale, and had then set to work settling his affairs.
Fortunately his pain had been slight, indeed he was
only bedridden for three weeks before he died, and in a
perverse way he relished the opportunity of structuring
his last months and arranging how Jenna's life would
proceed when he had gone. Any hope she had nursed
that he might be filled with an abrupt rush of love was
pointless. Edward was kind and friendly, he had always
been that, but he was distracted—he had always been
that, too.

Even the news, shortly before his death, that she was

pregnant was met with bland indifference. How inconsiderate of her! But now it was too late to rework his plans to include an offspring, that was Jenna's burden, so instead he continued writing long letters to his grateful constituents, meeting his bank manager for working lunches, and composing his own obituary. This morbid fascination with his own demise totally ignored Jenna and her state of mind.

'Please can we have some lunch?' Sarah was asking, and Jenna snapped back to the present.

The three children stood before her, eager for food, so she hastily set out the picnic. There was no more time for introspection, for now there were sandwiches to be eaten, squash to be drunk and sandcastles to be admired. Later they ambled down to the edge of the ocean for a paddle. It was Christopher's first experience of a warm sea and though he was tentative at first, dabbing in a toe, then running back squealing, in the end he was dancing in the waves and had to be dragged away. By mid-afternoon, however, he was beginning to fade, and when the thumb went into his mouth, sand and all, they packed up. Slowly they wandered home along the promenade. Sarah and Beth disappeared into their own house, and although Jenna called, 'Are you back, Sam?' the stillness of the rooms was proof enough that he was still in Sydney. She settled Christopher down for a nap and, after showering, decided to rest herself.

Noises downstairs awoke her and a glance at her watch showed she had been asleep for far longer than the cat-nap she had intended. Christopher was half awake, so she roused him, dressing him in his sleepsuit with the intention that as soon as the evening meal was over she would take him straight back up to his bed. The day's mixture of sun and sea had tired him and, with luck, he might now resume his regular stretch of twelve hours' sleep each night.

Jenna inspected her reflection in the wardrobe mirror. The sun had smudged her skin with a faintly glowing gold, and she chose a collarless button-through smock in cotton voile, deciding the pastel-green flattered her hint of a tan. After brushing her hair and applying a touch of mascara, a dab of perfume, she plucked up her son from where he was playing at her feet and went downstairs. She found Sam in the kitchen, competently assembling the ingredients for dinner.

'I was going to grill some fish!' she protested.

'You're too late, lazybones,' he said, grinning at her sleep-soft face. Christopher had his head on her chest, and when he murmured drowsily, Sam chuckled. 'You were both dead to the world when I looked in on you, so I thought I'd better get cracking. You can take over as head cook and bottle-washer tomorrow.' He lit the gas beneath a Chinese wok.

'What are you making?'

'Fried rice, Sam's style.' Deftly he stir-fried rice and sliced spring onions, adding handfuls of prawns, pork pieces and garden peas. 'I lived on it for months at a time in South-East Asia, so now it's a regular on my menu, but my speciality is squid with beansprouts.' He circled a thumb and finger, making a kissing sound. 'It's superb!'

There was one thing about Sam, Jenna decided wryly, fastening her son's bib under his chin, he displayed an infinite capacity for surprising her.

'Tomorrow evening we're going to a concert at the Opera House, I bought tickets this afternoon,' he said as they sat down to eat. 'And Marge has agreed to babysit.'

Jenna's winged brows lifted at this further surprise, then drew together. 'Suppose Vivienne wants to be interviewed tomorrow evening?'

'She won't. I telephoned her and apparently she's

taking time off to recuperate from the long flight. She'll be in touch in a day or two.' His fork paused on its way to his mouth. 'You'll be pleased to hear she's still hooked on the honest approach, so I reckon your article will be going ahead as planned.'

To allow her thoughts time to catch up with him, Jenna took a mouthful of fried rice. 'This is lovely!' she exclaimed. It was, too, a mouthwatering blend of textures and tastes. Sam really was an astonishing individual.

Although Christopher ate some food, he never came fully awake and as soon as they had finished Jenna took him straight upstairs to bed. When she came down to help Sam with the dishes she began prodding herself into the correct frame of mind to tell him about the traumas of her past, and why their relationship could not progress. But try as she might, she found it impossible to pluck up her courage. There was a mental block as far as offering him the painful truth was concerned, and by the time the dishes were dried Jenna had decided to leave her speech until the following day. She was aware she was acting the coward, but if she rehearsed overnight perhaps her confidence would grow. She was starting up with some harmless conversation when Sam took hold of her elbow and pushed her down on to the sofa.

'You have to explain your feelings some time,' he announced, as she took the glass of wine he was offering. 'I need to know all about your marriage. I need to understand.'

The way he was pre-empting her resistance disconcerted her.

'Can't we leave . . .'

'No, we can't,' he cut in. He sat down beside her. 'Start at the beginning.'

There seemed to be no escape. Nervously Jenna ran her fingers along the stem of her glass, and took a deep shuddering breath. 'I met Edward through my university course,' she began. 'A group of us visited his weekly surgery where he met constituents and dealt with their problems and complaints. Most of the other students faded away after a few weeks, but I admired his dedication to his work and continued to attend. Gradually I became involved.'

'And Edward fell for you?' Sam asked, taking a mouthful of wine.

She made a feeble attempt at a laugh. 'I don't think he actually *fell*, but my interest flattered him. He enjoyed having an adoring female around who was eager to discuss his work.'

'You adored him?' he asked.

'I thought he was wonderful.' Jenna remembered the cloud she had floated on when Edward had first noticed her. 'He was so urbane, so dignified. I was amazed when he showed a serious interest in me.' Her mouth twisted. 'And so was everyone else! My mother behaved as though Royalty had appeared on the scene, and although I took a lot of teasing from my friends, I could tell they were in awe, too. Edward was a whizz-kid in politics. He was frequently on television because he was so . . . so presentable. A rapid rise to positions of great power had been prophesied, and I'm sure my mother had me mentally installed at Number Ten Downing Street.'

Pushing his fingers into the opening of his shirt, Sam idly rubbed the tanned skin. 'But you were very young. Why, if he was such a catch, hadn't an older woman grabbed him years ago?'

'Anyone more mature would have realised he didn't have much to offer in the way of, of . . . personal commitment,' she said thinly, raising her eyes to gaze at the distant trees silhouetted against the orange ball of the sinking sun. 'He was kind, supportive about my writing, generous with his money, but . . .' she wafted a hand, 'he gave so much of himself to his career that there was nothing left over.'

'Why did you stay with him if you were unhappy?'

'Because I'd made my wedding vows,' Jenna said simply.

'And if he hadn't died you would have committed yourself to a lifetime's misery?' His voice was like cold steel.

'What reason did I have to leave?' she implored, setting down the untouched wine which was in danger of spilling with the trembling of her fingers. She pressed her palms together, seeking composure. 'Basically the only thing that was wrong in our marriage was the physical side, and that was partly my fault.'

'Why?' he demanded roughly, putting aside his own glass to catch at her hands. 'Why do you blame yourself?'

'Because I . . .' Jenna broke off. 'Because I was incapable of rousing him. He would turn away when I touched him or kissed him, he was indifferent to me. I left him cold.'

'Did he have other women?'

'No!' All of a sudden she was yelling, angry at Sam's lack of understanding. 'Edward was loyal.'

'Loyal!' The word was spat out like a plum-stone.

'Yes, loyal,' she insisted. 'I know he was too wound up in his career to devote much time to the physical side of our marriage, but if I'd had the right chemistry it could have worked.' She scowled at the look on his face. *It could!*

Sam muttered an oath. 'Some men don't need a woman very often, honeybunch,' he said, holding tightly on to her hands. 'No matter how alluring, how beautiful their partners, they don't respond to love-making.'

'But I didn't enjoy it either!' she cried. How could she make him understand? 'I just went through the motions, but nothing ever happened.'

'You enjoy it with me.'

'Yes, but only so far.'

Sam began to undo the buttons on his shirt, one by one, and she watched, hypnotised, as the sultry chest was revealed an inch at a time, contrasting with the brilliant white of the material. Now it was open to his waist, and he raised himself to pull it free from his trousers. He caught hold of her hand.

'Rub your palm against my skin,' he ordered softly.

Her hand tingled as he steered it on to his chest. She felt the grainy scour of sunbleached whorls of hair, the body warmth.

'No!' she gasped, turning away.

He caught hold of her jaw in his fingers and forced her to look at him. 'I never slept a wink last night wondering how I could get it through to you that you're not frigid, Jenna. And today I doubt I made much sense at my meetings, because my mind kept returning to you. The guys probably decided I was suffering from a hefty dose of jet-lag.' He gave a self-deprecating twitch of a brow. 'There's only one way to convince you that you're wrong, that your husband was at fault, not you. You need some sexual healing, honeybunch, so now we're going to go to bed.'

He rose to his feet and held down a hand to her. Jenna gazed at him, her heart thudding.

'Come with me,' he murmured tenderly, and she found herself rising.

Fearful anticipation coursed through her veins as she perched on the edge of Sam's bed and watched as he stripped off his clothes. At first she had kept her eyes down, but he was totally at ease, and gradually curiosity had got the better of her. He *was* a sun-god, for only a tiny patch of pale skin at his hips interrupted the golden length of his body. He had drawn the curtains and switched on a bedside lamp, and now in the subdued light his muscles rolled smoothly beneath his skin. Jenna had never seen a male body in such detail, for Edward had always scuttled into his pyjamas, believing nudity a sin. He had hated to be looked at, but Sam was relaxed, smiling at her fascination when she felt she should look away. But he's *beautiful*, she thought in wonderment.

'We'll take it step by step,' he told her, sitting down and taking her in his arms.

The feel of his warm nakedness, the male fragrance of his skin, made her heart thump unevenly. 'Painting by numbers?' she managed to joke, but her voice vibrated.

He bent to trace the outline of her half-open mouth with his finger. 'Yes, and when we reach a colour you don't like, we'll stop and find one that you do.'

Gravely Jenna looked into his face as he drew closer. 'I love you,' she said.

'Don't sound so surprised!'

The mischievous lilt in his tone made her smile, and suddenly the high-voltage cable which was wrapped around her snapped. She was laughing into his shoulder, her blonde hair brushing his skin.

'I love you, too,' he said, laughing with her. 'But then, because I'm ... brash, I've been telling you that for ages, haven't I?' She laughed again. 'That's better,' Sam murmured. 'If you're going to be seduced you might as well enjoy it.' He stretched down an arm. 'First we'll remove your sandals. It's crass to make love with your boots on. Colonials like me might do it occasionally, but the English? Never!'

'Oh, Lord!' she sighed, entering into his mood. 'And as we're in Australia do we have to sing regular choruses of "Waltzing Matilda"?'

'Full marks!' Sam chuckled. 'You're getting the hang of it already.'

Now Jenna was dangerously alive, super-sensitive to the touch of his hands on her feet as he unbuckled the ankle-straps and dropped the sandals to the carpet. He stroked her feet, pushing his fingers between her toes and pretending to nibble at them until she found herself wriggling down into the softness of the bed in a paroxysm of pleasure. Excitement surged as one by one he kissed her toes and then devoted himself to her insteps, making her giggle at the brush of his mouth on the skin. Next he caressed her ankle and worked all the way up to her knee. Jenna was short of breath.

He straightened to study her face, his brown eyes heavy with love. 'Now we'll go back to the top left-hand corner, like all good little boys and girls.'

Apparently her mouth had been designated as the top left-hand corner, for Sam pushed his fingers into her hair, holding her in position while he gently nibbled at her lips, kissing and teasing as he ignited a series of tiny yellow sparks that suddenly burst out of control into red-hot flame. Jenna twisted her arms around his neck to pull him closer, and his kisses became urgent. All gentleness had gone, but she no longer wanted gentleness, now she demanded his male strength, hungering for him with an unbeatable need which transcended the limits she had previously set. Her hands slid on to his shoulder muscles, her nails marking small crescents on the tanned flesh as her desire grew. Sam slid open the buttons of her smock and pushed it aside, and when she tilted her head to expose the smooth column of her throat and the thrusting swell of her breasts, he groaned. Fighting against a pitch of emotion which was in danger of overwhelming him, Sam made himself discover her body a step at a time.

'My lusty lady,' he murmured, his breath ragged.

She moved beneath him, the hairs on his chest rubbing across her breasts to create a giddying ecstasy.

'Love me, Sam,' she implored as he caressed the silky jutting peaks.

She was frenzied with passion, whispering his name in a broken voice as his mouth scorched her breast, and his limbs entwined with hers. Sam raised his head. He saw her pupils darken and darken, and he could wait no longer.

Afterwards Jenna was spent and demure. They lay for a long time sharing a luxurious afterglow as they whispered their mutual adoration.

'I didn't believe in love at first sight,' Sam murmured, touching her shoulder with the tip of his tongue. 'But whatever it was when I first met you, it was ...' He shrugged. 'The French have a phrase, *coup de foudre*.'

'Lightning,' Jenna smiled, feeling deliciously smug.

Languorously they started to caress each other again, and the excitement mounted.

'Oh, darling, that husband of yours didn't know what he was missing!' Sam groaned, his muscles clenching as she moved her hands over his chest. 'I only thank God you've saved all your love for me.'

She sighed and nestled closer, her fingers exploring the body of the beautiful man whom she loved, and who loved her. 'Do all your family have gaps?' she asked, pushing his lips apart to touch his teeth. 'Or is it an Australian characteristic? I seem to remember Mr Desborough-Finch has a similar disability.'

'Disability? Let me tell you it's a sign of *the* most virile men,' Sam grinned, sliding his hand against the satin hollow of her thigh. 'I'll prove my case tonight, my darling, and tomorrow we'll call and ask Kirby to give his confirmation.'

Jenna smiled, her lips against his shoulder. 'You would too, wouldn't you, my love?'

'Do I ever tell you lies?' he protested, all deadpan innocence.

An incoherent murmur came in reply. There was the urgent thrust of her body against his, burning skin, throbbing heartbeats, and an emotional tidal wave caught at them both, carrying them on its foaming crest until it tumbled to the shore, leaving them clinging together exhausted and replete.

## CHAPTER EIGHT

NEXT morning Christopher's shriek of dismay woke them.

'Mummy—where my mummy?' he was yelling, for he had toddled into Jenna's room and found it empty.

'In here!' she called, and he came running, happiness restored now that he had found her.

Scrambling on to the bed, he crawled over her, careless elbows and knees poking into sensitive places, and then hooted with delight when a tousled head emerged beside Jenna's. 'Daddy Sam!' he yodelled, bouncing up and down as they winced in unison.

'I reckon you can stick to "Daddy" in future,' Sam drawled, reaching to deposit a kiss on the corner of Jenna's mouth. 'Now that you've caught me redhanded there's only one decent thing for me to do, and that's to make an honest woman out of your gorgeous mother.' He moved his mouth over Jenna's, kissing her with a thoroughness which made her grow weak.

'Me want a kiss,' Christopher protested, forcing their heads apart with a flurry of determined hands. Laughing, she kissed him, and then he pushed his mouth at Sam to receive a second contribution. 'Tickle, tickle,' he beamed, poking stubby fingers into their necks.

Sam thrust one arm out of the blankets and tickled back, but the other slid on to Jenna. The combination of her son throwing himself gleefully around on top of the bedclothes and Sam's undercover fingers, gliding and stroking, snatched away her breath.

'I want you,' she moaned softly into his ear, nuzzling against the powerful physique which was showing signs of an answering arousal. This was one time when she would gladly have done without her son's presence.

Sam's lips moved into a smile against her cheek. 'Last night you were frigid and now you're insatiable!' he teased. 'And don't you *dare* move your hand any lower, otherwise modesty will force me to get out of bed.'

'Get up, get up!' crowed Christopher, and yanked away the covers.

'Thanks, Chris,' Sam said wryly, and headed for the bathroom.

'We'll drive into town this morning and see Kirby,' Sam said at breakfast.

Jenna's blue eyes danced. 'Why? To ask him to verify that a gap in the teeth equals virility?'

He squeezed her hand. 'After last night I don't think there's any doubt, is there?'

She gave him a flirtatious look. 'I'd better wait until tomorrow to answer that, I can't base a whole theory on a single night's activities.'

'Insatiable!' Sam declared once more, and leant across to kiss her. 'I can see we'll have to be married as soon as possible before I run out of steam and you have second thoughts. You might be a late starter, honeybunch, but at the rate you're going you'll soon catch up—if I live that long!' He became serious. 'Where are we going to base ourselves, Jenna? I *could* work out of London if you're keen to pursue your political writing.'

'No, thank you. This seems the perfect time to start out on my freelancing. I can come along when you're making films and take photographs and write articles on the same topics. But you'll have to teach me about nature, I've been a city girl so far.' Jenna grinned mischievously. 'If you teach me as efficiently as you've already taught me about the birds and the bees, I don't foresee any problems, do you?'

In answer he reached across to kiss her again.

'Kiss me,' Christopher demanded.

'Not while your mouth's inches deep in marmalade,' Sam demurred.

Jenna wrapped her fingers around her coffee cup. 'I'll give Herbert my resignation the minute I get back. I wonder how he'll react?'

'Ecstatic pleasure,' Sam decreed flatly.

'Actually it would be nice to call in on Mr Desborough-Finch,' she mused. 'He's been very supportive and I'd like to thank him for his help and explain why I'm leaving.'

'Right, that's fixed. First Kirby, then lunch, then I'll take the Boy Wonder off your hands while you buy yourself something exotic for our visit to the Opera House.'

Jenna arched a brow. 'You think jeans and flying-jacket would be out of place?'

'A little,' he grinned. 'Just a little.'


On arrival in the city centre Sam parked his car alongside a gleaming Rolls-Royce in what appeared to be private parking bays for the Desborough-Finch offices. Jenna chewed her lip, wondering if they had any right to be there, but the attendant greeted them happily, so she presumed Sam knew what he was doing. When he led them into a lofty vestibule she was as round-eyed and silent as Christopher, absorbing the hushed elegance, the fluted crystal chandeliers, the gold-leaf etching on white marble walls. Back home *The View*'s premises were well equipped and far superior to many other newspaper offices she had visited but were, nonetheless, a complete contrast to the displayed wealth of the international headquarters of the Desborough-Finch empire.

A well-groomed brunette, her hair swept up into a sleek chignon, was stationed behind the walnut reception desk, and she greeted Sam with a familiarity that rocked Jenna back on her heels.

'What a pleasant surprise, Mr Sam,' she said, smiling at him over half-glasses. 'Mr Kirby will be delighted.'

If Jenna was thrown off balance, Sam was completely at home—but, she realised, Sam was at home anywhere. When they took the lift to the penthouse suite another elegant receptionist, a cool blonde this time, had anticipated their arrival and she ushered them into a vast oak-panelled room.

Mr Desborough-Finch rose to greet them. 'Sam, my son,' he boomed, striding forward. 'How was the trip to Europe?'

'Fine, Dad.'

Jenna's mouth dropped open, but before she could assemble her thoughts Sam was introducing her.

'I believe you know Jenna?'

The tall, grey-haired man shook her hand warmly, and when he smiled she saw the gap in his teeth which he had passed on to his son.

'It's a pleasure to meet you again, Mrs Devine, or may I call you Jenna?'

'Jenna,' she echoed weakly.

'Please call me Kirby, Desborough-Finch is one hell of a mouthful. I can almost understand why Sam opted for something simpler.'

Words failed her as her eyes darted from one man to the other. Now it was blaringly apparent that they came from the same stock, though the older man was thicker-set, his face lined and weatherbeaten.

'And who's this?' Kirby asked, dropping down to Christopher.

The little boy's hand sought Jenna's. 'Me,' he whispered.

She pulled herself together. 'This is Christopher, my son. I've kept him a secret until now, and I must apologise. I know I was. bending company rules, but I can assure you my work has never suffered in consequence.'

Kirby straightened. 'I'm sure it hasn't. I read your columns to keep abreast of political developments, and you're a damn fine writer.'

'Thank you.' She was delighted by his praise.

'And she has lovely long legs,' Sam drawled.

'I had noticed. Why do you think I made a point of visiting when I was in London?' his father sparkled, and indicated a group of leather chairs around a low table. 'Let's sit down. I'll arrange some coffee and,' he nodded towards Christopher, 'fresh orange for the young man?'

Jenna held the glass carefully, determined there would be no accidents. The thick carpet was pale blue Persian and would not take kindly to a puddle of orange juice. Only when Christopher had drunk every drop could she relax. Sam grinned, reading her relief, and now that she was free, he announced, 'Jenna and I have come to tell you that we're going to be married.'

His father beamed and set down his coffee cup. 'That's wonderful news!'

There were kisses and congratulations, and when at last the older man's questions about where and how they had reached this decision had been satisfied, he sat back and grinned at Christopher, who was spreadeagled on the carpet, making zoom-zoom noises with a couple of paperweights and a cardboard box which had been discovered in Kirby's desk drawer.

'At last I shall have one handsome grandchild,' he said. 'All the Desborough-Finch variety are saddled with Roman noses and gappy teeth, poor little devils.'

'A most attractive combination,' Jenna said loyally, and a massive feeling of love suffused her as she shared a smile with Sam.

'Glad to hear you think like that,' Kirby returned. 'From the expression on both your faces I'd hazard a guess that you'll be producing your own brood before very long!'

Jenna took a sip of cofee to cover her confusion, but Sam just laughed.

'I shall be resigning from *The View*,' she explained, needing to be brisk and businesslike.

Sam's father frowned. 'I suppose that's inevitable, but it's a great loss. Even Holt will have a few misgivings.' When Jenna raised her brows in disbelief, he added, 'He speaks highly of your work, though he can never bring himself to forgive you for your gender. You don't fancy working for one of my newspapers in Sydney, do you?'

'No go, Dad,' Sam intruded, and there was the touch of the whip in his voice. 'You know where I stand on nepotism, and that includes daughters-in-law.'

Kirby sighed and turned to Jenna. 'This son of mine has some pigheaded hang-up about making his own way in life. His trip to Europe was the one and only time he's ever agreed to work for me, and that took all my persuasive powers!'

'You caught me at a weak moment when I'd been away from civilisation for months on end, and it happened to tie in with my visit to Scotland,' Sam inserted heavily.

'But look what you came back with! I take full credit for you meeting Jenna,' Kirby grinned.

'Okay, father knows best—*sometimes*!' Sam agreed, laughing.

His son's good humour made Kirby decide he could risk a minor offensive. 'So why don't you swallow your goddamn pride and agree to come into the business with me?'

The abrupt switch to serious discussion made Jenna realise that this was a subject which had been chewed over at length, with Kirby making little headway.

'I don't think so,' Sam said pleasantly, pushing his hair from his brow.

His father winked at Jenna. 'I suppose I must accept that that's progress, of a kind. Usually I'm told where to go in no uncertain terms! But nothing is ever fixed and final, maybe the influence of a wife and family will make him think again.' He raised a hand when he saw Sam's hackles begin to rise. 'Calm down, son. Let me telephone Susan and pass on the good news. I think a family get-together is called for, are you free this evening?'

'Sorry,' Sam said apologetically. 'We're going to the Opera House.'

'Then come out to the house tomorrow. I'll scrounge a day off work. Hell, it's taken you thirty-two disreputable years to get this far, so a day of riotous celebration is demanded! And later you must do the rounds of the relations and show Jenna off.'

'Er ... I'm in Sydney on business,' said Jenna. She could visualise Herbert's reaction if she dared to return with her work unfinished. 'I'm interviewing Vivienne Valdis, so I could be tied up.'

'Vivienne Valdis? What the hell are you interviewing her for? Politics is your forte.'

'It's Herbert's idea,' she explained. 'He swapped round the roles of some of *The View*'s journalists.'

Grinning at his father's air of outrage, Sam took up the tale. 'Before you bust a gut, it's working out fine. Jenna's showing Vivienne as a real person, not some blend of bosom and teeth, and all the signs are that the other writers are responding equally well to the different stimuli.'

Kirby nodded acceptance of the experiment, but refused to relinquish his hold on a family celebration. 'Bring the Valdis girl along to the house too, if necessary.'

'Don't forget I'm working as well,' Sam intruded. 'I have more photographs to organise. Just because I'm the proprietor's son it doesn't mean I'm prepared to wriggle out of my responsibilities.'

'I'm well aware of *that*!' his father growled, then he smiled. 'We'll work something out. Hell, *I'm* the boss and a prospective father-in-law, don't I have some say in the matter? The Valdis assignment can be fitted in,' he declared, batting away a triviality he refused to recognise as a problem. 'How long are you planning to be in Sydney?'

'Ten days.' Sam swapped a grin with Jenna. 'We hope to be married in roughly a month's time, so you'd better tell Susan that a trip to England is on the horizon. We'll have a few days alone in Scotland for our honeymoon, then the Boy Wonder,' he smiled down at Christopher still brum-brumming on the carpet, 'and the film crew will join us and I'll start the documentary. After that we'll base ourselves in Manly and look at life afresh.'

The conversation spiralled into questions and answers until Christopher lost interest in the makeshift toys and Kirby took them out to lunch. An instant rapport appeared to spring up between him and the little boy, and the meal developed into a two-way exchange of toddler-talk, much to Sam and Jenna's amusement. The shared lunch was enjoyable and Jenna was delighted to have the chance to get to know Kirby better, but equally she was burning to be alone with Sam and challenge him with her discovery that she was destined to become Mrs Samuel Desborough-Finch and not plain Mrs Sam Wood as she had imagined.

It was early afternoon when Kirby finally allowed them to depart, waving a fond goodbye to Christopher.

'Why didn't you tell me you were Kirby's son?' she demanded the minute the lift doors closed behind them.

'I didn't want you to marry me for my father's money.'

'Be serious, Sam!'

He inspected his watch. 'We're running behind schedule. Off you go. Christopher and I will meet you

back at the car around five.' He bent to kiss her cheek.
'All will be revealed in due time.'

Purely by chance Jenna discovered a small boutique in
a quiet square off one of the main shopping streets
which displayed the kind of chic clothes she had always
admired but, owing to Edward's conservative influence,
had never owned. Taking a deep breath, she dived
inside and tried on a variety of dresses, finally choosing
one in white jersey silk with a low scooped-out neckline,
full sleeves studded with hundreds of seed pearls, and a
softly swirling skirt. A narrow silver belt encrusted with
pearls encircled her waist, and when the dress had been
reverently wrapped and paid for, she swung happily off
along the street, congratulating herself. Never before
had she chosen anything so seductive and so prettily
feminine. Minutes later a pair of silver slingback
sandals caught her eye, and silver shimmer tights,
filigree bracelets and pearl choker were swiftly added to
her purchases. A glance at her watch showed time to
kill before she was due back at the car, so Jenna spent
the remainder of the afternoon having her ash-blonde
tresses styled by a mincing young man in tight pink
jeans and a fringed waistcoat.
    'You look beautiful, darling,' he simpered, holding
up the hand mirror for her to inspect the back view,
and Jenna laughed out loud when Sam repeated the
identical sentence minutes later. He walked around her,
eyeing her unusual sophistication, for her hair had been
drawn up into an elaborate gleaming knot at the back
of her head.
    'And me beautiful,' Christopher piped.
    'And you,' she agreed, her eyes travelling between her
son and Sam in surprise. 'You've both had your hair
cut! You do look smart, and different.'
    Christopher's silver-white curls had gone. Now he
was a proper little boy with a neat bob, a straight fringe

across his brow. She felt a twinge of dismay; her baby had gone!

Sam placed his arm around her shoulders and gave her a squeeze. 'They all grow up sometime, you know, honeybunch, but you'll be having more.'

Jenna gulped away the lump in her throat, revived now at the prospect of bearing Sam's children. 'Did he yell blue murder?'

'He was perfect. I sat him on my knee while the barber cut his hair and told him more about the kangaroo from Warrumbungle.'

'Warrum . . . bungle!' spluttered her son.

'The other customers were fascinated,' Sam said drily. 'You do realise that's my reputation as a hardbitten cameraman gone down the drain! No one's going to believe I'm either tough or intelligent any more.'

Jenna chuckled, then she ran her fingers across his collar. 'The barber's floor must be knee-deep! All your blond has disappeared.'

He flipped back the crisp, surprisingly dark hair from his forehead. 'That was just Jenna-catching gear. I'm really no more than mouse, very ordinary, but now that I've trapped you I can afford to revert to type—my glass eye and wooden leg go back into their cases tonight.'

'I bet the nose is false, too, and the teeth.' She tilted her head, grinning impudently. 'No, no one in their right minds would fashion teeth like that, unless there was an acute shortage of white plastic!'

Sam placed his hand on the supple curve of her waist and dragged her against him. 'Be careful, when I bite your neck I shall be marking you as *mine!*'

Although Jenna was itching to discuss his true identity it was impossible to find time to talk, for after a speedy drive back to the house there was a meal to prepare, Christopher to put to bed, and then she was busy showering and dressing for the evening ahead.

'My beautiful lady,' Sam said huskily, when she went downstairs to join him.

A cloud of Je Reviens floated around her, and the soignée hairstyle and softly swirling dress added a fresh dimension to her charm. He placed his hands at her waist and smiled down, his brown eyes gentle with love.

'I'm not the type to make flowery speeches, but somewhere up in the heavens it was decreed that you and I should meet. We're made for each other.' For a moment he was seized with the need to make her his again. 'All I want to do is make love to you, Jenna. Worship you in the only way I know, show you how much I care.' He looked deep into her eyes, joining the two of them together, heart against heart, soul entwined with soul. 'I love you, and you look absolutely divine.'

'A very classy couple,' a bubbly voice intruded, and they wheeled guiltily apart as Marge came into the room. She grinned, sensing she had intruded on a special moment. 'My word, Sam, I've never seen you looking so smart!' Recovering his aplomb, he stood to laughing attention as she listed his attire. 'Brown velvet jacket, trousers with razor-sharp crease, cream frilly shirt and bow tie. Don't let Barry see you, otherwise he'll develop an inferiority complex!'

Jenna watched the teasing with a smile. Sam looked so debonair, a true Desborough-Finch! But although the handsome man-about-town cut a striking figure, she was reluctant to forget the dishevelled sun-god who had first claimed her heart.

Outlined against the mellow evening sky, the Opera House had a magical quality. Surrounded on three sides by softly lapping waves, it was a splendid twentieth-century palace, its doors flung wide to welcome the throng who had come to pay homage to the performing arts. Jenna held on to Sam's hand, alert to the impressive auditorium, the glamour of her surroundings. Although their fellow theatregoers were smartly dressed, she decided *they* were the best-looking couple there, totally without bias, of course! It was impossible to ignore the women who registered Sam's lean physique, and she was aware of several male eyes appraising her as well.

'Thank God you belong to me,' Sam whispered when one young man gave her a particularly frank once-over. The pressure of his fingers on hers made her melt to marshmallow.

The concert was given by a brass band. A blast of trumpets opened the show, and from then on it was good music all the way. The repertoire ranged from classics to jazz to swing, even to the latest hit songs from the Top Twenty, and then the band leader had only to hint before the audience joined in, clapping and singing. The more exuberant numbers were interspersed with piano solos and slow tempo numbers. The performance passed all too soon, and as the final note rang out the audience rose *en masse* shouting for more. Two encores were greeted with thunderous applause, but eventually the ovation died away, and the concert-goers surged out down the long sweep of shallow stone steps into the night.

'Do you want to go dancing at the Wild Cockatoo?' Sam asked with some diffidence.

Jenna shook her head, smiling at the half-hearted gesture. 'I'd rather go home.'

He squeezed her hand. 'I can't wait to get into bed with you,' he purred.

She gazed innocently back. 'But I don't want to go to bed, I want to talk.'

Marge stayed for a few minutes to hear about the concert, then gathered up her knitting and left.

'Why didn't you tell me you were Kirby's son?' Jenna demanded, as Sam poured two goblets of brandy.

Tossing away his velvet jacket, he sat down beside her, staring into the golden liquid as though seeking an answer. 'As I told you, after my father's second marriage I wanted nothing more to do with him, but Kirby has a reputation throughout the world, and the name is so distinctive that whenever I introduced myself I was promptly classified as his son and heir. Before anyone knew the first thing about me, I'd been pigeonholed as a wealthy playboy, living on Daddy's money.' His lip curled in scorn.

'Did being a Desborough-Finch bother you before the quarrel?'

'Not in the slightest, it was open sesame to living in the limelight, and collecting a mass of girl-friends.' He gave a wry chuckle. 'Hell, who would refuse the heir to the Desborough-Finch fortune? But at the back of my mind I was never quite certain whether it was me they craved or the money.' He grinned impudently at her over the top of his goblet. 'At least as Sam Wood I knew it was my body they were after!'

'Have you had many ... lovers?' Jenna asked carefully, though she had already guessed the answer.

'Enough, but never anyone I wanted to marry.' He reached to caress the back of her neck, his fingers gliding over the smooth skin. 'Wood seemed a simple workmanlike name, so I adopted it.'

'Did you change by deed poll?'

'No. I'm still Desborough-Finch in my passport. I just began using the name Wood when I returned here from South-East Asia, and it stuck. I was determined to make my own way in life without any help, conscious or otherwise, from my father.' The corner of his mouth lifted. 'He owns a fair slice of the media in Sydney, so I was thrown to the opposition. I knew damn well they'd be chary of employing a Desborough-Finch, so I called myself Wood.'

'But did no one find out?'

'Yes, in time. Too many people knew me from the past for it to remain a secret for ever, but by then I'd proved my worth as a cameraman and my bosses realised I was my own person. My identity became one of those secrets everyone knows, in Sydney at least.'

Jenna took a sip of brandy, the liquid flaming her throat. 'Does Herbert know who you are?'

'Naturally. Didn't you detect a ring of deference in his attitude towards me? Privately he considers I'm an Aussie bastard, but to my face it's all smiles. Why do you imagine he made the empty gesture of appointing me head of our little assignment?'

'I thought he was hitting out at *me*!'

Sam grinned. 'Perhaps he was killing two birds with one stone.'

'And what's Kirby's reaction to the different surname?' Jenna asked thoughtfully.

'He hates it. He regards it as a sign of immaturity in me.'

Her retort was crisp. 'He's right!'

With a low growl of protest, Sam made a lunge and scooped her up into his arms, kissing her with such mock ferocity that their brandy goblets were tipping precariously.

'Whose side are you on?' he asked, setting the glasses aside and reaching for her again, his mouth warm and avid in the low neckline of her dress.

Jenna cultivated a mask of cherubic innocence, though it was impossible to deny the voluptuous electricity which was rich in her limbs from Sam's onslaught. '*Your* side, darling.'

'You'd better be,' he insisted, teasing the zip at the back of her dress, moving it down and up, and down. He pushed aside the jersey silk to stroke the snake of her spine. 'Fight me, honeybunch, and you'll soon discover who will come out on top.'

'Not me?'

The zip slid further down.

'Not unless I decide I like it that way.'

'But why didn't you tell *me* you were Kirby's son?' she persisted, struggling to ignore the desire he was intent on arousing.

He sighed. 'Initially because I didn't see that it made any difference.' He leant forward to brush his lips against her throat. His mouth was half open, his breath sweet and hot against her skin. 'Then ... well, I guess old habits die hard. I applied the same standards to you which I applied to girls in the past. I admit to a hang-up about my father's wealth and I was frightened that if I told you the truth I'd never know whether it was me you were interested in, or the money.'

'But I *wasn't* interested in you.'

'You liked what you saw,' he slammed back wickedly. 'You might not admit it, but you fancied me from the start!'

Jenna sighed. 'The modesty of the man!'

'We were destined for each other, you know that. Otherwise how come our two halves make up into such a delicious whole?'

Large eyes dancing, she pouted in reply. Sam bent to catch the pouting lower lip between his teeth, sucking gently, then with a moan, his mouth parted on hers and he pulled her against him, his hard body against hers, strong and demanding. The zip was ripped open and the dress pushed from her shoulders. He unpinned her hair, his kisses hot on her skin as they shared the tender truces of passion. Clothes discarded, their bodies fused, flesh into flesh, as he brought her inexorably to a height of desire she had never reached before. Now she knew she was part of him.

'Love me, Sam,' she sobbed, desperate for an end to the exquisite torture and yet not wanting it to stop.

'Here, or in bed?' he murmured, his mouth engulfing a fiery nipple.

'Here—*now!*' she moaned imploringly, her body moving against his.

He was devouring her, and yet, as he pulled her down beneath him on to the rug, she needed to give him more of herself.

'*Jenna!*' His voice was thick, his eyes glazed.

She was moving impulsively, her fingers clutching into his hair, pulling at his shoulderblades as she arched against him, giddy from the wonderful torment. His muscles were tense beneath the golden burning skin, his kisses covering her body. Jenna was panting, a film of perspiration on her brow as she accepted and returned his love. Her heart thudded against his in a ragged pagan beat, and suddenly the years of frustration swelled into one joyous outpouring as Sam took her violently, crying out her name and grinding her beneath him. Heart stopped, she clung to him as he took her to a land where all was touch and feel and sensation. Her groan of fulfilment joined his and they toppled headlong into dark warm wonderful space.

A wisp of grey smoke drifted from the chimney of the whitewashed cottage nestling in the cleft of the Scottish Highland valley. Overnight the storm had subsided and now the world was at peace, the heather-covered hillsides tranquil beneath the weak golden rays of a wintry sun.

Sam opened the front door and looked up into the sky. 'Come on, honeybunch,' he called. 'A brisk walk down to the village will tone up our muscles. Honeymoon or not, we can't stay in bed twenty-four hours a day!'

Fastening her flying-jacket, Jenna came to stand by his shoulder. 'Why not?'

A merry glint sparkled in his brown eyes. 'Now that you mention it, I can't bring one single decent reason to mind.' He made as if to unbutton his sheepskin jacket. 'Shall we get back between the sheets?'

She laughed, reaching up to kiss him. 'Not just yet, there are two good reasons for going out. One, so that I can telephone Mrs Millet and check on how Christopher is surviving and, two, in order to buy a copy of *The View*. Don't forget the first part of the Vivienne Valdis article is featured in the colour supplement today.'

'Words by Mrs Desborough-Finch,' he grinned, recalling Herbert Holt's bewilderment when he had learned of developments.

'And photographs by *Mr* Desborough-Finch,' Jenna returned, slipping her hand into his. 'Just as a passing thought, I seem to remember that one reason for us choosing to come up to Scotland was for you to make final arrangements for your documentary—whatever happened about that?'

'Some woman sidetracked me,' he said, deadpan.

'Is that what you call it?'

Sam gave a throaty chuckle. 'I can think of far more descriptive words. Shall I tell you exactly what the hussy did to me? Here, I'll whisper.' By the time he had finished Jenna was bright pink and weak at the knees.

'I have a nasty suspicion you'll always be able to shock me,' she said.

'I damn well hope so!'

Although the air was cold and the earth hard beneath their boots, the pace Sam set made the blood pound and by the time they reached the village Jenna's face was pinkly glowing—with exercise this time. A solitary phone box stood on the main street, and they squeezed into it, though not without difficulty, for Sam was rather large in his jacket. He moaned with exaggerated pleasure as she wriggled into position.

'We'll have a shot at making love in one of these, some day.'

'We will not!' She pushed his hand away. 'Behave yourself!' Hastily she dialled the number, giggling when he pushed his face into her hair, whispering saucy locations for lovemaking. 'Mrs Millet? It's Jenna here.' Suddenly she was serious, and Sam restrained himself. 'How's Christopher?' There was an interval as she listened intently, then he saw her relax. There was some general talk, a confirmation of their return to collect the little boy two days later, and when she replaced the receiver she was all smiles.

'Everything fine?' he asked, though he could tell it was.

'Apparently your father and Susan have taken charge, so Christopher's off at the seaside with them today and they're going to some toy fair tomorrow. He'll be in seventh heaven with his new granddad.'

'And get spoilt to death. If I'm not careful I'll be passed over and the Boy Wonder will be groomed to take control of the Desborough-Finch empire!' Sam eased himself out of the telephone box.

'But you reckon not to be interested in your father's business,' Jenna teased, as they walked along to the newsagents.

'In those few spare moments when you aren't having your way with me,' he fended off a punch, 'I've been considering his proposition that I have a trial period at the Sydney offices and discover what's involved, no strings attached. What do you think?'

'I think you should make up your own mind.'

Sam sighed. 'I knew you'd say that. Don't you want me to be able to afford to drape you in silks and satins, mink coats and diamonds?'

'No.'

He stopped in his stride, pulling her against him. 'Well, you damn well ought to, young lady. Where's your avaricious streak?' He tilted his head. 'I'm haunted by fantasies where you're lying on silver fox fur, your legs sprawling out for ever from beneath a white lace negligé. How can a poor cameraman afford all that?'

Jenna grinned. 'But you'd only take the negligé off and we'd end up where we always end up.'

He growled deep in his throat.

*The View* purchased, they walked home and while Jenna made mugs of hot coffee, Sam stoked the fire. Sitting together, they pored over the article.

'It reads well,' he said at last, his eyes meeting hers in mutual pleasure. 'And the photographs are fine.'

'Thank goodness Vivienne stuck with the truth, I'm sure it'll pay off in the long run. She even agreed to allow her correct age to be published!'

'Another geriatric,' he scoffed.

'It was a painful admission, ageing six years overnight must have been harrowing.'

He put his arm around her shoulders. 'I didn't notice you shedding copious tears when you reached thirty a couple of weeks back.'

'I hardly noticed it,' she admitted. 'But I have other things on my mind.'

'Such as?'

'Such as my son and my career,' she retorted.

'And?'

'That's all,' she said with a great show of innocence.

'You've missed someone out,' said Sam, his grip tightening. 'I'd better jog your memory.'

'And how do you propose to do that?' she asked, smiling at the love in his brown eyes.

'I'll think of a way, believe me.'

She did.

# *Harlequin* Plus

## A WORD ABOUT THE AUTHOR

Although her first novel wasn't penned until she was nearly forty, Elizabeth Oldfield actually began writing professionally when she was a teenager. She had enrolled in a writing course taught by mail. As guaranteed, the course more than paid for itself with money she subsequently earned from sales of her writing to magazines and newspapers—but at that stage of her life, writing was really only a hobby. Soon other types of work outside the home and family life took her away from dreams of living by her pen.

After a number of years of marriage, her husband, a mining engineer, was posted to Singapore for a five-year spell. Here Elizabeth enjoyed not only exciting leisure activities — tennis, handicrafts, entertaining fascinating visitors from all over the globe—but also the opportunity to absorb as much as possible about a culture as varied as it was exotic. And having more time on her hands, she resumed her writing—once again finding success at articles, interviews and humorous pieces.

But she had a larger goal: to write a book. Romance novels caught her eye. By the time she left Singapore, she had completed two novels and eventually saw both published—sending her on her way as a romance novelist. Now she works four days a week on her books, spending the rest of her time in various activities, including, whenever possible, hours spent with her family.

# Just what the woman on the go needs!

# BOOKMATE

### The perfect "mate" for all Harlequin paperbacks!

### Holds paperbacks open for hands-free reading!

- **TRAVELING**
- **VACATIONING**
- **AT WORK • IN BED**
- **COOKING • EATING**
- **STUDYING**

Perfect size for all standard paperbacks, this wonderful invention makes reading a pure pleasure! Ingenious design holds paperback books OPEN and FLAT so even wind can't ruffle pages—leaves your hands free to do other things. Reinforced, wipe-clean vinyl-covered holder flexes to let you turn pages without undoing the strap...supports paperbacks so well, they have the strength of hardcovers!

*Snaps closed for easy carrying.*

Available now. Send your name, address, and zip or postal code, along with a check or money order for just $4.99 + .75¢ for postage & handling (for a total of $5.74) payable to Harlequin Reader Service for to:

**Harlequin Reader Service**

In U.S.:
P.O. Box 52040
Phoenix, AZ 85072-2040

In Canada:
649 Ontario Street
Stratford, Ont. N5A 6W2

MATE-1

# Yours FREE, with a home subscription to
# SUPERROMANCE™

Now you never have to miss reading the newest **SUPERROMANCES**... because they'll be delivered right to your door.

Start with your **FREE** LOVE BEYOND DESIRE. You'll be enthralled by this powerful love story...from the moment Robin meets the dark, handsome Carlos and finds herself involved in the jealousies, bitterness and secret passions of the Lopez family. Where her own forbidden love threatens to shatter her life.

Your **FREE** LOVE BEYOND DESIRE is only the beginning. A subscription to **SUPERROMANCE** lets look forward to a long love affair. Month after month, you'll receive four love stories of heroic dimension. Novels that will involve you in spellbinding intrigue, forbidden love and fiery passions.

You'll begin this series of sensuous, exciting contemporary novels...written by some of the top romance novelists of the day...with four every month.

And this big value...each novel, almost 400 pages of compelling reading...is yours for only $2.50 a book. Hours of entertainment every month for so little. Far less than a first-run movie or pay-TV. Newly published novels, with beautifully illustrated covers, filled with page after page of delicious escape into a world of romantic love...delivered right to your home.

# Begin a long love affair with
# SUPERROMANCE
## Accept LOVE BEYOND DESIRE **FREE.**

## Complete and mail the coupon below today

- - - - - - - - - - - - - - - - - - - - - - - - - - - - - -

# FREE! Mail to: SUPERROMANCE

In the U.S.
2504 West Southern Avenue
Tempe, AZ 85282

In Canada
649 Ontario St.
Stratford, Ontario N5A 6W2

**YES,** please send me FREE and without any obligation, my
**SUPERROMANCE** novel, LOVE BEYOND DESIRE. If you do not hear
from me after I have examined my FREE book, please send me the
4 new **SUPERROMANCE** books every month as soon as they come
off the press. I understand that I will be billed only $2.50 for each book
(total $10.00). There are no shipping and handling or any other hidden
charges. There is no minimum number of books that I have to
purchase. In fact, I may cancel this arrangement at any time.
LOVE BEYOND DESIRE is mine to keep as a FREE gift, even if
I do not buy any additional books. 134 BPS KAMU

| NAME | (Please Print) |
|------|----------------|

| ADDRESS | APT. NO. |
|---------|----------|

| CITY | |
|------|--|

| STATE/PROV. | ZIP/POSTAL CODE |
|-------------|-----------------|

SIGNATURE (If under 18, parent or guardian must sign.)

SUP-SUB

This offer is limited to one order per household and not valid to present
subscribers. Prices subject to change without notice. Offer expires September 28, 19